real actors, not people

A Frannie Shoemaker
Campground Mystery

by Karen Musser Nortman

Cover Design by Aurora Lightbourne

TABLE OF CONTENTS

CHAPTER ONE

MONDAY AFTERNOON

THE TOWERING PINES lined both sides of the gray road. Their looming shapes emphasized the persistent storm. Each bump in the rural road was magnified by the thirty-foot trailer Frannie Shoemaker and her husband Larry pulled behind their truck.

Frannie leaned forward in the cab of the truck and peered through the slapping windshield wipers, using the pines to help pick out the road's gray shoulder. "Yeow!" Frannie felt like her ribs had punctured her lungs, and she gripped the door handle with white knuckles.

"Sorry," Larry, said as their red Chevy Silverado jolted along the highway.

"Are we getting close?"

"It should be coming up on your left—maybe just beyond that next curve. Ooof." She bounced again.

Larry grimaced. "Do you know for sure or are you just guessing?"

"I'm guessing." She scrutinized the atlas in her lap again and rubbed her sore ribs.

"Boy, setup is going to be fun in this mess," Larry said.

"I was afraid we'd been too lucky with the weather on this trip. Time to pay the piper. But I am so ready to stop and get off this road." Frannie's phone chirped. She looked down at the incoming text from her sister-in-law, Jane Ann.

GPS says one mile ahead on the left.

Frannie relayed the message to Larry. "We either should get a GPS or have someone else lead."

"Let's have someone else lead."

"I see the park sign!"

Larry turned on his blinkers and slowed for the turn. The driving rain camouflaged the actual entrance until they were right on it. He pulled in slowly. A narrow road wound back to the park's campground entrance. At the check-in station, Larry pulled over to the side and parked. Their traveling companions, the Ferraros and the Nowaks, pulled in behind them.

The Shoemaker's old yellow Lab, Cuba, sat up in the back seat as soon as they stopped.

"You'll have to wait a few minutes, girl," Frannie told her.

"Where are our raincoats?" Larry asked.

"In the trailer."

"I was afraid of that." He rummaged around in the back seat and pulled an old jacket out of a pile. He threw it over his head, got out of the truck, and jogged for the check-in shack. Mickey Ferraro and Rob Nowak were right behind him.

Fifteen minutes later they returned to their vehicles. Larry found a rag under the seat and mopped his face.

He hung the yellow reservation tag on the rear view mirror.

"I was hoping that by the time we checked in, the rain would be letting up, but no such luck there." He put the truck in gear. "Let's go find our site and get this over with."

"Water first," Frannie said. "There's no water hook ups at the sites."

"Damn. Forgot that already. The ranger did say that water and the dump station are up that hill." He pointed behind the guard shack.

Larry led the little procession up a short hill to a large open area with two sets of water hoses and dump facilities. He pulled up to one and Mickey the other, with Rob waiting his turn.

Frannie picked up the camper keys from the truck console so she could open the trailer to monitor the water gauge while Larry filled the tank. "I'll get your slicker, too."

She ran back to the trailer's door, unlocked it, and unfolded the steps. Inside, she pulled on her own raincoat and grabbed Larry's. He had followed her and gratefully put it on, pulling the hood up, and heading back out.

While the tank was filling, Frannie returned to the truck, put Cuba on her leash, and let her out of the truck to do her duties. The dog wasn't anxious to stay out long and was soon ready to return to the truck. Frannie went back to the trailer to watch the water gauge.

3

Once they had the tank full, Larry left his water hose hooked up for Rob and pulled ahead to wait. He and Frannie sat in the truck, damp and clammy, and tried to get a look at the surrounding park.

Ojibway Falls State Park, on the Upper Peninsula of Michigan, was the group's fourth stop on their UP tour. The park included thousands of undeveloped acres, spectacular waterfalls, and two large campgrounds. As retirees, the group could take a leisurely tour of the UP in September to enjoy the fall color. They planned a five-night stay in order to get a good look at the park. If the rain continued, it may not be much of a look.

Once everyone had water, Larry again led the way on a winding road back to the campground. The group had three adjoining sites reserved. The set up was as miserable as the water fill had been.

Larry and Frannie were still getting used to slightly different set up procedures. They had traded their old travel trailer for a brand new one that summer. This one featured a more spacious floor plan and amenities like a power awning and a built-in fake fireplace that doubled as a space heater. But there were enough differences that they weren't comfortable yet with the processes. They'd already had to replace the water pump—not a good omen.

Finally, all three units were level, stable, powered, and snug against the storm. By that time, dark had descended. They had planned to gather at the Shoemakers' trailer, so Frannie towel-dried her hair and the dog, changed her socks, and put out some crackers and cheese.

She had just poured herself a glass of wine when Mickey and Jane Ann pounded on the door and let themselves in.

"Why didn't we look for a tavern where we could hang out until this was over?" Mickey complained.

Larry handed him a beer. "What if it lasted for three days?"

"I don't see a problem."

"Big talk, Ferraro. Your days of an all-night bender passed you by about twenty years ago."

The Ferraros sat together on the couch, and Frannie threw Jane Ann a fleece blanket. "You look cold."

Jane Ann nodded, her teeth chattering, and snuggled under the blanket. Rob and Donna Nowak arrived, with the same weather-related complaints. Donna was a short, stocky woman with blonde, spiky hair. Her abrasive manner had been difficult to adjust to. But after several camping trips, Frannie had to admit to herself that Donna had a good heart and didn't mean some of the offensive things that she said in the way they sounded. She was also very disorganized.

"Frannie, I brought some salsa. Do you have any chips?" Like that. Donna never had everything she needed.

"I'll get some." Frannie went to the pantry cupboard, located a half-full bag, and poured them in a basket. "We decided we're each doing our own leftovers tonight, right? You could bring them over here if you want to eat together."

Jane Ann said, "Thanks for the offer, but I feel a cold coming on. I think I'll be ready to just tuck in, watch a little TV, and go to bed."

"It's been a long day," Donna agreed.

"We made too many stops." Mickey dunked a chip in the salsa. "We don't have to hit every antique store in the UP, you know."

"There's no such thing as too many antique stops," said Jane Ann.

Mickey gave up and pulled up the weather forecast on his phone. "Looks like this mess will move out in the night. Tomorrow should be pretty good. Want to hike to the Lower Falls?"

"I'm up for it," Frannie said. "On the park website it says there's supposed to be a wooden walkway the whole way, so we won't have to worry about mud."

They discussed breakfast plans, and the Ferraros and the Nowaks headed back to their own campers for the night. Frannie was glad no one wanted to do any more. She wanted a hot shower, but didn't want to go back out in the rain to the shower house. With a five-night stay, they would need to conserve their own fresh water for dishwashing and toilet flushing.

After a supper of warmed-over beef stew, she got into her flannel pajamas and curled up with a blanket and a book while Larry checked the news on his iPad. His efforts at tuning in the TV only produced two clear stations with nothing they were interested in. It was an early night for both of them.

CHAPTER TWO
TUESDAY MORNING

THE NEXT MORNING, Frannie, as usual, got up before dawn. She plugged in the chrome percolator that she had prepared the night before and checked the weather on her laptop. Mickey was right; the rain had moved out and the temperature was supposed to be in the high 60s with a few scattered clouds. Much better.

Cuba got up from her spot on the floor, stretched, and laid her head on Frannie's knee.

"Outside?"

The dog danced around, clicking her toenails on the vinyl floor.

"Relax. Let me get my shoes and jacket."

Since it was still dark, she turned on the outside light and led the dog along the parking pad to avoid the worst of the mud. A big security light lit the campground road. There were a few other RVs scattered through the campground, but it was by no means full. Across the road and down a steep cliff, the Ojibway River provided a soothing background mumble to the peaceful setting. But she kept her eyes open and the dog close, in case the bear warnings on the park website were true.

After their little walk, she snagged an orange-cranberry muffin, polished off another cup of coffee, and gathered her shower supplies.

It was getting light, and the shower house stood only a few hundred feet from their camper. A covered walkway separated the individual showers from the bathrooms. Her criteria for good campground showers began with at least two hooks, and preferably more, for her clothes and towel. A curtain separating the shower from the dressing area to keep those clothes dry was an added plus. These showers had two hooks but no curtain. She gave it a B+.

As she walked back to the camper, finger-combing her short salt-and-pepper curls, she passed a campsite festooned with yard ornaments and a sign that read 'Campground Host.'

A tall thin woman with dark-rimmed glasses and graying hair watered the flowering pots. She looked up. "Good morning! Quite a storm we had last night." She put down her watering can and walked over to Frannie.

"It sure was, and I swear we were setting up in the worst of it."

The woman looked up at the sky. "I'm Madelyn Mays, by the way. And as you can guess, my husband Chet and I are the hosts. Well, I'm certainly glad it moved out—we have a slew of people coming in today."

Frannie was surprised. "On a Monday? Is it a rally or something?"

Madelyn laughed. "It's going to be something, all right. They're going to film the pilot here for a new reality show called Celebrity Campout. Oh, I hope I can count on you not to call the media — they've been keeping it pretty hush-hush, and I'm not supposed to say much." She covered her mouth and winked.

"Wow. Celebrity campout?"

"I think most of the celebrities are has-beens or never-weres, if you get my drift. The production company has made a slew of last minute demands, so I'm expecting a lot more headaches. They're bringing in ten luxury motor homes this morning for four days. Their idea of 'roughing it.' They'll be over in that loop." She waved her hand toward the area on the other side of the bath house.

"I've never watched any reality shows — what do they do?"

"I don't know for sure, but I think they usually have some kind of competition and then stir things up to get a little drama going. We'll see. Just don't post anything on Facebook or anywhere, okay?"

"I won't. Is it okay if I tell the rest of my group?"

"Sure. They're going to know anyway in an hour that something weird is going on."

"We're planning on walking over to the Lower Falls after breakfast so we probably won't be around for a while."

"Oh, that's a great hike, and the falls are beautiful. We've had more rain than usual this fall, so the flow is pretty good too. I'd better get ready for the onslaught. Have a great day!"

"You, too," Frannie said and continued on her way.

Mickey was outside starting a campfire. He had already hauled out plastic totes of firewood, his grill, and a lawn chair.

"Hey, gorgeous! Looks like a better day today." He grinned. She had rarely ever known Mickey to be grumpy or out of sorts. The last time he was, they thought he was having a heart attack.

"Yup. You were right with your uncanny weather predictions."

He lowered his voice. "Don't tell anyone, but the Internet helps."

"Any sign of Larry yet?"

"Nada. And I need some coffee."

She laughed as she went up the camper steps. "Well, don't ask him, or you'll get another lecture about making your own. I'll bring the pot out."

She went in and checked the bedroom. Larry still nestled under a mound of blankets, but she could tell by his restlessness and occasional snorts that he would be awakening soon. She unplugged the coffee pot and carried it outside. Because of the rain, they hadn't set up any of their usual outdoor accessories the night before, so she got a small side table out of the storage compartment and set it by the outdoor outlet for the coffee. After plugging the pot in, she turned back to Mickey.

"There you go, mooch. You have to provide your own mug. Jane Ann up yet?"

"Yeah, she's getting dressed. We need to talk about breakfast."

"Absolutely. We wouldn't want to starve. I'll wipe the table off and get a tablecloth. Be back in a minute."

She found an old bath towel, got her coffee mug and a tablecloth, and Cuba's leash. When she returned outside, Rob had come over and Jane Ann did some stretches. She stopped and helped Frannie with the table.

"Boy, do I have some gossip." Frannie settled in her lawn chair with a full mug of coffee. She filled them in on the reality show.

"Wow!" Mickey put down his fire stick and stood up. "I always wanted to be on TV."

"I don't think they're holding tryouts, Mick. It's called Celebrity Campout. As famous as you are in our circle, I doubt if you'd qualify."

Jane Ann turned from pouring her coffee. "Now, you've crushed him, Frannie."

"So who are these celebrities?" Rob asked.

"The host—Madelyn—described them as 'has-beens and never-weres.' But she didn't say who. I don't know if she knows."

"Ah, well," Mickey said, "Fame is a fleeting thing. But breakfast is a different story. I thought I'd do an omelet in the cast iron."

"I think breakfast is pretty fleeting around here. I'll fix sausage," Rob said. "I've already got my little gas grill set up."

Larry made it outside just in time for breakfast and some pointed comments by Mickey. They were still seated at the picnic table when they heard a rumble, soft at first but getting louder, coming from the campground entrance. The first motor home through the gate looked like it would barely fit and the one behind it looked even larger. Even more incongruous was the golf cart gaily leading the pack.

"It's like one of those Star Wars movies where the space ship passes over and never ends—just gets bigger," Mickey said, as he turned in his seat to watch the parade go by. "The drivers don't look like celebrities."

Frannie shook her head. "The way Madelyn told it, those RVs are rentals being delivered."

The man in the golf cart—probably Madelyn's husband—jumped out when the vehicles arrived at the other loop. He began directing the motor homes into sites one at a time. Two Suburbans arrived and began picking up the drivers as they completed their parking chores.

Rob looked at the others and smiled. "Who do you suppose is going to hook up all of those? And do you think they filled the fresh water tanks first?" Now they watched the man from the golf cart gesturing to one of the drivers, who adamantly shook his head. He held out a clipboard to the host, who also shook his head.

"That might be what the discussion is about," Larry said.

"Seems like if the celebrities are going to experience camping, they should be doing the setup," Jane Ann said.

Donna rested her chin on her fist, with almost a dreamy look on her face. "I wonder who the celebrities are."

No one else expressed much interest, but they continued to watch the real reality show unfold. Finally, there seemed to be some agreement, and the drivers who hadn't already parked returned to the RVs and followed the golf cart back out of the campground.

"Water," Larry and Rob said, in unison.

The drivers who had already parked helped the host hook up several hoses to a water spigot near the shower house and began filling the three RVs one by one.

Frannie stood up and began to pick up dishes. "If we're going to hike this morning, I think we should get a move on."

Mickey saluted. "Yes, boss." They each carried their food and dishes back to their campers.

THEY DECIDED TO TAKE Rob's truck for the short ride to the trail head to save time. By the time they were ready to leave, the rest of the motor homes were parked, and the host went from one to another, plugging them in and putting out the slides.

"He doesn't appear too happy," Jane Ann commented.

Mickey chuckled. "Can't you just imagine how this went? Someone who never camped came up with this scenario and arranged for a bunch of rentals, assuming all you need are a few RVs."

Rob nodded. "Oh yeah. This could be really good entertainment for the next few days."

They reached a large parking lot and extracted themselves from the truck. An asphalt path led uphill to an observation deck. The river far below the deck tumbled and roared in a manner quite unlike the docile waters that passed the campground farther downstream. Across from the deck, an island split the river, and the elevation change created spectacular waterfalls on both sides of the island.

Mickey examined a map of the park that he had picked up from a kiosk. He smoothed it on the railing and glanced from it to the vista laid out in front of them. "The path is that boardwalk off to the right, and it leads to those falls over there." He pointed to the right. "To get a good view of the ones on the left, it looks like you have to rent a row boat and row over to the island."

"Where do you do that?" Rob asked.

Mickey put his finger on the map. "There's a boat rental right off the board walk. We can either do that when we get back or wait until later."

"They don't have a ferry or a motorboat or something to take you over to the island?" Donna asked in a petulant tone.

Mickey patted her on her head—an action that resulted in a flat spot on her spiky hairdo. "No, my precious. We have to use our own muscles. But it isn't that far."

He led the way to the boardwalk while Donna used a comb to repair her hair.

Jane Ann glanced over the railing as they ambled along. "I see why they put in a boardwalk. It looks like nothing but swamp below us."

The thick woods did seem to be seated in mud and shallow water. Ferns added to the tropical swamp feeling, unexpected in the north woods, but as they raised their eyes, the beginning fall color of birches and maples belied that impression. Towering pines were interspersed with other hardwoods that occasionally leaned over the walkway. Between the treetops and the ferns below, understory trees and shrubs provided a mosaic of shapes, textures, and shades of green, brown, and yellow. Sunlight played through the branches on their right, while the tumbling river could be glimpsed through the trees on the left.

"What a beautiful place." Frannie breathed deeply. "If the waterfall is as impressive as the walk, it should be quite the sight."

They met others coming back—a few families with young children, but being a weekday, most of the visitors were in their age range.

The path wound around the bend in the river, and in no time the roar of the falls signaled their nearness.

CHAPTER THREE

THE BOARDWALK TURNED toward the river and widened into a large deck overlooking the falls. Benches lined the downstream railings. Signboards on posts displayed information about the water flow, the flora and fauna, and the history of the region. The falls were not tall, but wide, and in places the water produced copper-colored froth — a result of the tannins in its bed.

Jane Ann and Rob snapped pictures.

"Let's get one of our group," Donna said. "Rob, do a selfie." She herded them into the corner of the deck with the falls behind them. After three attempts, Rob pronounced it a done deal.

They hung over the railing, mesmerized by the tumult.

"What is it about waterfalls?" Frannie asked no one in particular. "I can't pass one up, and I can't look away. It's not like it's changing dramatically, but they're just fascinating."

"The power?" Mickey said.

"Maybe. Look!" Frannie pointed above the falls. "Someone in a canoe!" A young woman drifted toward

17

the falls. As they watched, she deliberately dumped the craft and started swimming frantically for the shore. The canoe sped up and seemed to hurl itself toward the precipice. Larry and Rob rushed to the end of the deck and picked their way down the rocky bank.

The woman very slowly made some headway, but appeared to be tiring. She looked to be in her twenties or thirties, but it was difficult to tell because a mass of curly red hair engulfed her face.

Rob waded out in the current, while Larry held on to one of his hands. Rob reached. He yelled. She spotted him but was being pulled down river.

"Ohmigod!" Donna said. Jane Ann thrust her bag and water bottle into Donna's hands and ran to join the men. Frannie followed her and yelled to Mickey, "Call 911!".

When they got to the bank, Frannie and Jane Ann joined hands and Frannie put one arm around a tree. Larry grabbed Jane Ann's hand and moved into the river to give Rob more reach. The woman still struggled to swim toward them—at least, she didn't appear to panic. With the added length of the human chain, she grasped Rob's hand. As he pulled, she struggled to her feet, and he helped her toward the shore.

Jane Ann and Larry reached out to bring her the rest of the way. She collapsed on a large smooth rock, and Jane Ann helped her lower her head to the ground. She gasped for breath.

Mickey leaned over the railing of the deck. "The ranger's on his way."

Larry wadded his now wet jacket up and put it under the shivering woman's head. He looked up at Frannie. "Can I have your sweatshirt?"

She unzipped her hoodie and handed it to him. He used it to cover the woman's torso. Rob climbed up the boardwalk and started jogging to meet the ranger.

"Good job for him. He's a lot younger than us," Mickey said.

Donna leaned over the railing, too. "What can we do? Anything? Do you want to move her up to the walk? Does she need CPR?"

"Jane Ann's a nurse," Mickey muttered to her. "She'll know what the woman needs."

Donna was a little abashed. "Oh. Right."

Jane Ann was, in fact, monitoring the victim's pulse, and looked up at them. "I think she's going to be fine. She just needs to get warmed up."

The ranger arrived in a Gator with Rob riding in the back. They wrapped the woman in heavy blankets and got her seated in the Gator. She gave them a weak smile and thanked them. The ranger executed a neat three-point turn, and headed back to the main lodge.

Mickey pointed down at the canoe. It was wedged under the deck among the rocks, and creased in the center. "Good thing she got out of there."

"What was she doing?" Donna asked. "Surely, she wasn't going to try and go over?"

Larry gave her a 'back-off' look. "We didn't ask. She needed to get her breath back, not answer questions."

"Oh. Right."

"Ready to head back?" Rob asked. "I could use some lunch."

"Absoluuutely!" Mickey led the way.

BY THE TIME they reached the parking lot, the ranger was there in his Gator. Even if he didn't recognize their faces, Larry and Rob's wet clothes gave them away.

"Hey! Thank you folks for helping out!"

Larry stopped by the Gator. "No problem. How's she doing?"

"I think she'll be fine as soon as she warms up. An ambulance was waiting when we got here. It was a close call, though. Glad you were on the spot."

"What was she doing?" Rob asked.

The ranger scratched his chin under his short, red beard. "She said she meant to get out and portage but didn't know how close she was to the falls." His expression said he didn't quite believe that. "We get a lot of foolish mistakes here. Are you staying in the campground?"

"Yes, we are," Mickey said. "It's a beautiful park."

'Thank you. Well, I hope you have a good stay." He climbed back in the Gator.

As he drove away, Frannie said, "He didn't sound real sure that we would."

Mickey looked around at the wet clothes. Frannie had gotten her hoodie back but she was still shivering.

"Maybe we should wait for another time to row to the island."

"Ya think?" Larry said. They headed for the truck.

"You don't need to get sarcastic." In spite of the chill, though, she felt tremendously relieved that this incident had turned out okay. They had encountered enough tragedies in their camping days that any mishap now filled her with dread.

As THEY ENTERED the campground, they could see lots of activity by the motor homes. Several young men and women scurried around with large cameras on their shoulders. Some appeared to be actually filming scenes of the campground; others were in heated discussions with clipboard-bearing individuals.

"Maybe that's why the ranger wasn't sure we would have a good stay," Larry said. "I don't even see any 'celebrities' yet." He gave the term air quotes. They all piled out of the truck and stood watching for a few minutes, and then decided their lunches would be more interesting.

When Frannie came back out to the picnic table with her sandwich, Mickey had several brochures spread out.

"What are all of those for?"

"There's a couple of great-looking road trips here. There's a shipwreck museum on the lakeshore—about thirty miles from here, it looks like. And you can take a glass-bottom boat tour of some of the wrecks!"

Larry swung his leg over the bench and set his plate down. "Sounds appropriate for you. I thought you were so hungry — where's your lunch?"

"Oh, Jane Ann's making some ham salad. Thought I'd look these over and stay out of her way."

"We should all be so lucky," Larry said.

Donna came back from the shower house. She plopped down on the picnic bench, bursting with news. "I ran into one of those camera women in the bathroom. She says that one of the celebrities coming is Tommy Pratt!"

The others looked blank. Then Frannie put her sandwich down. "The old child star? He was in all those movies with the Shetland pony when we were kids?"

"He's not dead?" Mickey said.

"Apparently not. He's probably about your age, Larry," Donna said. "Isn't that exciting? A real movie star!"

Larry frowned but kept his mouth shut, knowing that everything Donna said should be taken with a grain of something. Jane Ann came out with plates for herself and Mickey.

Madelyn, the campground hostess, walked by leading a beautiful collie. They waved, and she led the dog over to their table. Frannie introduced Madelyn to the rest of the group. Cuba got up from under the table and put her nose on Frannie's knee, in case her mistress became too entranced by the visitor.

"We're just discussing the 'celebrities' coming." Frannie grinned as she did the air quotes that were becoming a habit any time someone said celebrity. "How are things going?"

Madelyn threw up her hands, almost losing the leash. "It's going to be a long few days. I hope the park is getting a lot of money off this. Their latest request is that, once they start filming, we ask the other residents of the campground to stay inside. Can you believe that?"

"What in the world are they worried about? Are they afraid someone is going to moon the camera?" Rob asked.

Madelyn laughed. "I think it's a payment issue. If you become a part of the film, they might owe you money. Chet, my husband, told them to edit anyone out they didn't want in it. That most people are here to be outdoors."

"Oh, brother," Jane Ann said. "I don't envy you this week. When are they supposed to arrive?"

"Later this afternoon. I think they will be brought in by bus." Madelyn shrugged. "We'll get through it, I guess. We really like hosting here. Into each life, a little rain must fall."

Mickey got up and stacked up his brochures. "You'd think we got enough of that yesterday."

"You're right. Better finish my walk before those people come looking for me."

"What's your dog's name? She's—he's?—beautiful." Frannie said.

"She. And it's Lassie, of course. Our grandkids had been watching the old TV shows, and they insisted. Yours looks very sweet, too. So well-behaved."

"Cuba," Frannie said, "and she's quite old. She doesn't have the energy to misbehave."

As if to contradict, Cuba raised her head and gave a short bark.

Madelyn laughed, waved goodbye and tugged the collie after her. "C'mon, girl."

Frannie absently stroked Cuba's head. Cuba counted on humans being absent-minded most of the time. Her human watched Madelyn go while she considered the whole phenomenon of reality shows. Was she just too self-centered to care about what happened to someone on an island or to a handsome young man supposedly looking for the love of his life—or formerly famous people trying out camping in an orchestrated setting? Something must be wrong with her.

"So after lunch, I'm all for a little nap. Stressful morning," Larry said.

It was a popular suggestion. They weighed other options for after naps and decided to go back and row to the island.

"The brochure says the hike around the island is only about forty-five minutes. That'll leave plenty of time for supper prep. I'm doing a meatloaf in the Dutch oven— you guys take care of sides," Mickey said. "Then maybe tomorrow morning or afternoon, we could check out the shipwrecks."

"Sounds like a plan." Frannie yawned. "Meanwhile…"

"Sleep tight," Jane Ann said.

She did. She took her book and fleece blanket back to the bed and curled up. She opened the blanket but not the book.

CHAPTER FOUR
LATE TUESDAY AFTERNOON

A YOUNG MAN of about twenty manned the boat rental. His name tag said 'Rick.'

"Have any of you rowed a boat before?" He looked doubtful.

"Many times," Rob said.

Rick selected two boats at the end of the row. "See that cement area below the dock?" He pointed to the end of the island about three hundred feet across the river. "Just pull the boats up there and tie them to that railing. Don't go below the buoy over there to the left or above that little riffle on the right, okay?"

He held the first boat and Rob, Donna, and Frannie got in. Rob volunteered to row and got no argument. The others took the second boat and designated Mickey the rower. The trip was easy, and Rob expertly piloted his boat toward the landing. Mickey's boat took a more circuitous route because he lost track of where he has headed while talking. Rob and Frannie had gotten their boat pulled up and tied and watched Mickey correct his course again while Larry yelled at him.

By the time he managed to hit the landing, Jane Ann couldn't wait to jump out. "I'm not riding back with those two."

"I'm rowing when we go back," Larry declared.

Above the landing, a weathered dock led to a set of stairs up the steep bank. When they got to the top, a path led in both directions. Other than the path, the island was thick with trees, especially pines.

"The falls we saw this morning are to the right, so let's go left." Mickey pointed. "The island is the only place you can get a close look at those falls."

"At least with a path, it'll be harder for him to go in circles," Larry muttered.

The hike was spectacular. Just enough crisp in the air to enhance the brittle blue sky and enough warmth from the sun to keep the chill off. The trail was well maintained, surfaced with crushed rock and edged by wood. It led along the river to another rock ledge with a railing overlooking the eastern falls. These falls were two tiered and not as high as those on the other side of the island, but pretty in their own right.

Frannie waved her arm toward the opposite shore. "I love it when the trees just start to turn in contrast to the evergreens. I don't think I've ever seen so many different kinds of pines."

"It is stunning," Jane Ann agreed.

They continued on, stopping to take pictures of the smaller falls and riffles that bordered the small island. Before long, they were at the south end, and the path curved back north to follow the other branch of the river. There were bird and wood duck houses occasionally but no benches or other comforts for humans. Frannie got the feeling that the message was 'Look, but don't stay long.'

"There's the other falls ahead," Rob said. They reached an observation spot, but no deck. Across the roaring river, they could see the broken canoe still wedged under the deck they had been on that morning.

While they watched, two men walked out on the deck, talking heatedly, but stopped for a moment transfixed by the sight. They returned to their conversation, which still appeared to be angry. One man, in a gray hooded sweatshirt, pushed the other, a tall guy in a cowboy hat, in the shoulder and stomped off the deck back to the path.

"Wow," Frannie said. "I was afraid we were going to witness a murder, or least another dunking."

Mickey grinned at her. "Frannie, let's try and make it through this camping trip without any murders, okay?"

"It's not my fault, Mick. Maybe *you're* the one that attracts all the crime. I just have to solve them."

"Talk about a pointless argument," Larry said. "Let's move along."

"Maybe there's a curse on this river," Frannie said.

Each turn as they continued around the island produced a new vista—a different combination of water, sky, and trees. Larry insisted he was going to row back.

Mickey agreed. "Fine with me. Then I can yell at you."

However, they made it back to the boat rental without any violence. Mickey declared that it was time to get back and start supper. No one objected to that either.

At the campground, Frannie went in the trailer to cut up the zucchini, red peppers, and yellow squash that she would sauté with a little onion in the cast-iron skillet over the fire. Mickey organized his cooking table to bake his meatloaf. Donna and Jane Ann worked together on a fruit salad.

Frannie came back outside in time to see a chartered tour bus circle the campground road and stop at the rental encampment.

Rob stood up from his task of building a fire and stretched. "Looks like the 'celebrities' have arrived." As people descended from the bus, the driver began pulling luggage from the lower compartments. Passengers claimed multiple-pieced sets of matched suitcases, lugging them toward the motor homes under the direction of a small, stout woman wearing a red baseball cap. Her hair was either short or all tucked into the cap.

One scruffier-looking couple made do with a large duffel bag but the rest appeared equipped for several weeks of festive events.

Larry looked at Frannie. "How long are they going to be here?"

"I think Madelyn said four days."

He shook his head and went back to helping Rob with the fire. Jane Ann and Donna appeared with a big bowl of fruit salad, and the group continued with their supper preparations, stopping occasionally to check out their own private live drama. After the luggage had been stowed in the motor homes, the participants gathered back outside for a meeting with Ms. Red Baseball Cap.

"I wonder what they're doing for food," Rob said.

Mickey scratched his head. "Maybe they have to *forage* for it?"

Larry laughed. "So they'll have grilled raccoon and pine cone soup?"

"After supper we should — you know — take the dogs for a walk. And in the process, get a closer look at what they're doing," Frannie said.

"Good idea," Jane Ann said. "Very sneaky."

"She is that," Larry agreed.

Donna clasped her hands. "Wonder if they need any extras. Wouldn't that be cool, to be on a TV show?"

"No!" the rest chorused.

Donna laughed. "You guys have no spirit of adventure."

"Frannie brings us way more adventure than we need when we're camping," Mickey said.

She huffed. "I object. But I'm hungry."

They sat down to meat loaf, sautéed veggies, fruit salad, and fresh bread.

Rob said, "Speaking of adventure, Ferraro, what are your weather prognostications for the rest of the week?"

Mickey stabbed a second slice of meatloaf. "Looks pretty good except maybe some light rain or mist on Thursday."

"So maybe we should do the shipwreck tour tomorrow?"

"Fine by me."

"I want to go to the Upper Falls, too," Jane Ann said.

"We can do that in the afternoon. Or in the morning and the tour in the afternoon." Mickey pushed back his plate. "What's for dessert?"

"Nothing." Jane Ann smirked at him.

Frannie said, "I have cookies in the freezer we can have later—after our walk."

Mickey wiped his brow. "Frannie, you are a lifesaver."

She rolled her eyes as she carried a stack of plates toward the camper. They decided to leave the dish washing until morning—"to save water"— and grabbed jackets to ward off the growing chill. They led the dogs first over by the river to view the beautiful sunset and then took off around the campground.

As they neared the rental motor homes, Larry said, "Look at that. That's how they're 'foraging.'"

A large refrigerated truck was parked along the road. People were coming out with what looked like packages of meat and bags of vegetables. One woman approached Ms. Red Cap. Her long blonde hair didn't look exactly natural and neither did her smooth face.

"How are we supposed to cook this?"

Ms. Red Cap stuck her pencil behind her ear and cocked her head. "You know there's a stove in the motor home, right? And there should be a grill in one of the

31

compartments." She pointed at the large doors at the bottom of the motor home. "Remember, you're *camping*." She smiled in an apparent effort to jolly the woman out of her funk.

Nothing doing. The woman stomped away without reply.

"Close your mouth, Donna," Rob whispered to his wife.

Donna clamped her jaw shut and then whispered back, "I think that's Amber Gold."

Larry said, "We'd better keep moving. Who the heck is Amber Gold?"

"She was the neighbor in that comedy about the family who were in witness protection — you know."

"I guess I don't. Let's go."

"You're kind of grumpy, Larry," Donna said.

Mickey laughed. "He's always like that."

Others were starting to gather around Ms. Red Cap, clamoring with questions. Two camera people moved around the crowd capturing the drama. Ms. Red Cap held up her hands and pointed back toward the center of the loop. "Folks! Calm down. Ted is setting up the social table and bar over there. How about everyone get a beverage, and we'll talk about meal procedures."

Mickey raised his eyebrows as they moved down the road away from the group. "They'd have been better off to stock those RVs with TV dinners."

Jane Ann agreed. "They don't seem very well organized. Maybe the 'social table' will help."

On the other side of the road, Frannie noticed a tall man clad completely in Western gear from a cowboy hat pushed back on his head to a plaid shirt, tight jeans, and cowboy boots. He was slender, except for a belly hanging over his belt that was a challenge to the shirt. He leaned with one hand on an oak trunk looking down and talking earnestly to woman with a pile of blond curls anchored to the top of her head.

Donna grabbed Frannie's arm. "I think that's Cooper Wainwright!"

Frannie raised her eyebrows. "And he is — ?"

"Country singer. He was on *Hee-Haw* or *Hootenanny* or one of those. shows. He only had one big hit that I remember — 'Saw-Horse Sadness.'"

Mickey hooted — but quietly. "You're kidding! The one about his girlfriend who painted farm scenes on saw blades and went off to the big city?"

"That's the one." Donna grinned.

"I do remember him, sort of. Always thought his name was kind of funny. In the old days, a cooper was a barrel maker and a wainwright was a wagon builder. Obviously a stage name," Frannie, the retired history teacher, said.

"So who's the woman, Donna?" Jane Ann asked. "Good thing we brought you along."

They had stopped on the road while Mickey knelt to retie his shoe.

"That might be his ex-wife, Tassi Ketchum. She tried the music scene and didn't score. For a while, she was on

33

one of those morning talk shows. I wonder if they're getting back together?"

Larry frowned. "Let's move on before we get arrested for stalking."

"I can see how including a couple of exes in a show like this could provide some fireworks," Rob said as they continued their walk.

Donna, however, twisted back. "Doesn't look like fireworks. He just kissed her on the cheek."

"The plot thickens," Mickey said.

CHAPTER FIVE

TUESDAY NIGHT

THEY GOT BACK to their site, stoked the fire, and were comfortably discussing their trip so far, when Ms. Red Cap suddenly appeared out of the darkness. She still carried her clipboard and took a seat on the picnic table bench. Up close, Frannie couldn't think of any way to describe her except 'plain.' She seemed all one color: wisps of beige-y hair stuck out from her cap; light eyes, beige eyebrows, and colorless lips all blended together. Her attire of a gray tee-shirt under a dark green windbreaker with jeans was just as nondescript.

"People, I saw you over by our area, and I'm going to have to ask all of you to sign an NDA."

Larry sat up in his chair, and his annoyance was clear on his face. "Excuse me—you are who?"

"Oh." Punctuated by a fake little laugh. "I'm sorry. Brandee—with two e's—Tudor. I'm the assistant producer for *Celebrity Campout*. As I said—"

"Wait a minute," Mickey jumped in. "What's an NDA?"

She sighed. It obviously took extra patience with these rubes. "A Non-Disclosure Agreement. You cannot reveal or publicize anything that you observe during the filming." She pulled several sheets of paper from the clipboard and counted them out.

"Are you kidding?" Larry stood up and faced her, hands on hips. "This is a public campground—a state park!"

Frannie put her hand on Larry's arm. "Larry, calm down." Usually he was the stable one, and *she* would fly off like a stepped-on cat.

Rob crossed his arms and leaned back in his chair. "I'm not signing anything."

Jane Ann shook her head. "I don't see why we should. We aren't planning any big expose or anything. We've had reservations here for months. We have as much right to be here and look around all we want as your TV show does."

Ms. Red Cap—or rather Tudor—was beginning to lose her composure a bit. "But, you can't even post on Facebook or Twitter—you know what *that* is, right?"

"Of course," Mickey said.

She looked rather frantically back toward her encampment. "Anything that you reveal will spoil the show. We can't have someone give away what is going to happen!"

"Lady," Mickey said, "Even if I cared, I still wouldn't do it. When I read a book, I don't post the solution to the murder on Facebook. All you have to do is ask us nicely. We don't need any silly agreements. And you really have no right to ask us. We are minding our own business."

"But, my boss says I have to get these signed. Otherwise, we'll have to bring in the park manager."

"Wooo," Rob said. "Like sending us to the principal?"

Brandee Tudor got up. "Obviously, I'm wasting my time." She stalked off.

They looked at each other, perplexed. Finally Frannie said, "What just happened? I didn't even get to throw in my two cents!"

Larry looked toward the rentals. Brandee Tudor walked up to a man in a grey hooded sweatshirt and began to talk rapidly, pointing back toward them and throwing up her hands.

"Tattletale." Mickey got up to put more wood on the fire. They watched as the man put his hands on his hips, shook his head, looked over at them several times, and then headed their way.

Rob looked around their little circle. "We need to add a lawyer to our group."

The man in gray arrived. "Good evening, folks. I think my assistant got off on the wrong foot with you. May I?" He gestured toward the bench.

"Certainly," Frannie said.

"I'm Cliff Remboski, the director of *Celebrity Campout*. You see, we're trying to produce a pilot for a new reality show, and it's really crucial that word of the content does not get out before we're ready."

Larry nodded. "We understand."

"You do? But Brandee said—"

"Ms. Tudor walked up and demanded that we sign these papers without introducing herself or explaining what they were for."

"Really?" He looked back at his site where Brandee stood waiting. His silver, perfectly-styled hair belied the effect he tried to give with his ripped jeans and frayed sweatshirt. "Well, I'm very sorry about that—it's been rather hectic this afternoon."

Remboski was so well spoken that Mickey put on his retired English teacher persona. He leaned forward in his chair and clasped his hands.

"May I ask, what is your premise? What are you trying to achieve?"

"Like most reality shows, we want to put people in unfamiliar situations and see how they react. Most people think that a luxury motor home is just like staying in a hotel."

"But for your cast, it is," Frannie said. "You parked and set up the RVs. You brought in a truckload of food. Not much 'camping' there."

"Wait and see," Remboski said and smiled. "Can I count on your discretion? I would prefer that you sign the NDAs, but you seem like honest people, and I'm sure you understand the need for secrecy."

Mickey said, "No offense, but we are not big reality TV fans, and we have plans for our stay here that will keep us pretty busy. We'll stay out of your hair."

"That's all I ask. Thank you. Have a great evening." He got up and walked away.

"He looks familiar," Donna said. "He must be somebody famous, too."

Frannie snapped her fingers. "That's one of the guys who was arguing on the deck this afternoon. You know, when we were on the island."

Rob nodded. "You are absolutely right. He sure didn't seem argumentative just now."

Jane Ann sat forward in her chair. "And the other guy on the deck was the country singer, I bet! He had his back to us, but same build and hat."

"As Mickey says, the plot thickens," Frannie said.

Mickey had gone in his camper and came back out with his guitar. "I think we need a little music to sooth the savage — um, atmosphere."

"Great idea!" Frannie got up. "I'll get the cookies and a little beverage."

By the time she came back out with a bag of gingersnaps and a glass of wine, the whole group was engrossed in watching the reality camp.

She opened the bag and offered it around. "Now what's happening?" She followed their stares and saw people milling around carrying heavy bags. Cliff Remboski appeared to be trying to organize them in a line. Soon they moved out, down a path into the woods.

"Maybe it's a snipe hunt," Rob said.

Mickey put down his guitar. "Be back in a minute." He jogged over to his camper and returned with one of the brochures he had picked up. He spread it out on the table and planted a stubby finger on one spot. "This is a park map and we're here. That path goes back to some back country campsites. That Remboski said 'Wait and see' when you told him they weren't really camping, Frannie. Maybe after letting them think they're staying in those motor homes, they're going to make them set up their own tents and really rough it."

"I bet you're right. Sometimes you're smarter than you look, Mick," Larry said.

Mickey slapped him on the shoulder, causing a wince. "Hey, thanks, buddy. You're too kind."

"We won't be able to see any of it," Donna said.

Larry smiled. "No, we'll be able to enjoy ourselves. Let's hear that guitar, Mickey."

CHAPTER SIX
WEDNESDAY MORNING

THE NEXT MORNING, Frannie was puttering around in the trailer when she heard loud shouts coming from outside. She raised a shade and peered out. It was beginning to get light, but no one was out in their area. She kneeled on the couch so she could get a better look around the camp ground. Over in the reality site, it looked like Cliff Rembowski arguing with another man. But someone shorter, definitely not the cowboy.

As she watched, Mickey came out of his camper and walked over to the road to check out the noise. She grabbed her jacket and joined him.

"What's going on?" she asked, as she walked up behind him.

"Not sure. I wish they'd move closer so I could hear what they're saying." He grinned sideways at her. "Kind of rude, dontcha think, not to let us in on the conversation?"

"It certainly is. Where're their manners? Can you tell who it is?"

He moved back toward the fire pit to work on the morning's blaze. "No, the guy's had his back to me the whole time. The only thing I heard was something about those 'stupid tents'. I'm thinking that these folks weren't told what they were actually going to be doing."

"Can they do that? I mean, they apparently have contracts."

Mickey bent over to light the kindling. "If they are mostly has-beens, they may be so desperate for a comeback that they'll sign anything."

Frannie hooked up Cuba's leash. "So maybe we're lucky that we've never been famous?"

"You are so right."

She took the dog over toward the river. An observation deck protruded out from the steep bank and stairs led down to a ravine where a small but determined creek emptied into the river. They stood on the deck for a few moments, enjoying the view. The rising sun highlighted the tops of the trees on the opposite bank. Yellows and light reds danced among the dark green spiky pines and provided a lush background to the tumbling river. A cardinal flitted from branch to branch in an elderberry bush near the deck, garnering Cuba's interest. She looked up at Frannie as if to ask "Can I have that?"

Frannie shook her head and drank in the overwhelming peace of the scene, in spite of the contentious voices in the distance. At the moment, she wondered how people could be so angry in these surroundings, but deep down she knew it wasn't such a puzzle. Disappointments, changes, losses—any number of bumps in the road—can make one's vision so constrained that everything else is lost from view and anger takes over. Human nature.

But this — this kind of setting at this hour of the day — was one of her favorite things about camping. And these 'celebrities' didn't and probably wouldn't appreciate that. The vision of Ms. Brandee Tudor leading them to the riverbank to watch the early morning sun like a first grade field trip made her chuckle.

She led the Lab back to the campground road. They passed several single campers, some with people out cooking breakfast, others still quiet. She reached the rental encampment. No one was out, including the two men who'd been arguing earlier. All was quiet. Across the road a path led to the tent sites, according to Mickey.

She looked back at her camper and didn't see Larry outside. He would think she was being nosey, but this path was part of the park, right? As silly as she thought the reality show idea was, she wondered about how the group got through the night. She didn't know how far the tent area was, but it would be a change from their usual walk, and she could always turn around. They headed down the path.

It was easy walking on the path surfaced with sawdust and wood chips. Cuba found interesting smells along the edge. The trees filtered the sunlight like a natural, gentle strobe light. She was just thinking that she should go back and fix herself some breakfast when she smelled campfire smoke. They continued around the next bend in the path and found the walk-in tent area.

It wasn't exactly chaos, but it some ways it reminded Frannie of one of those old engravings of one of the circles of Hell. Some of the tents appeared to be standing only with good intentions, and several people sat around on campstools or logs, their faces the perfect picture of 'Abandon all hope.' None of the voices were happy.

The smoke came from an attempted campfire. The woman who had been talking to the country singer the night before—Tassi?—crouched near a fire ring, fanning a pile of leaves and crumpled paper that had been placed on top of some logs. Good thing that Mickey and Larry weren't there to offer their critiques.

"Trouble?" Frannie said to the woman. Tassi glanced up and looked around. Frannie now noticed one of the camera people over by a group of four who were trying to fix breakfast without much success. No one seemed to have yet realized that an outsider lurked in their midst.

"Yeah," she said softly. "Trying to get this damn fire started."

"Would you like some advice?"

The woman stood up and wiped her hands on her jeans. "Yeah, sure. Cliff told me he would help,"—again she looked around to see if anyone was listening—"but I haven't seen him."

"Cliff? The producer?"

Tassi nodded.

"He was back by the motor homes earlier. But I'll be glad to help. You need to start with the paper on the bottom, and find some small sticks for kindling." She looked around the site and picked up several sticks. Tassi watched her a moment and then apparently decided that it would only be polite to join in. Frannie used a larger stick to pull the mess in the fire pit apart and push the paper back into the center. She piled the sticks on the paper, and Tassi did the same.

"Do you have a lighter?" Frannie asked.

The woman produced a cigarette lighter from her pocket. How in the world she got it in the pocket of those tight jeans, Frannie didn't know.

"Now light the paper," Frannie said. "Then add more sticks until the sticks are burning, not just the paper. *Then* add your logs."

"Thank you. I'm sorry now that I ever got into this. Nice dog."

Cuba had been sitting, watching the humans with the same puzzlement that she usually did.

"Thanks. She's a sweetie, usually. Why *did* you get into it?"

"Coop thought it would help me make a comeback. 'Course, he also thinks we should get back together. That isn't going to happen. I don't see him around when I need help, either."

"I'm sorry — it can be frustrating at times, but we have had some great moments camping. Good luck."

The woman nodded. "I'll need it."

Frannie led the dog back to the path, and they returned to the main campground. She hadn't spotted Cliff Remboski or Brandee Tudor, but it seemed at that point a good idea to keep moving before somebody made her sign something.

Back at their campsite, Mickey contemplated the fire. Frannie went in to get a bowl of cereal and brought it back out to join him.

"Solving the problems of the world?"

Mickey stirred himself. "What? Oh, yeah, I guess."

"So what are you so deep in thought about?"

He grinned. "How did the world get so screwed up? I mean, you just ended a sentence with a preposition. What's with that? And, this whole manufactured 'reality' thing. If they would just ask us, we could tell 'em all how to run things." He stirred the fire and put another log on.

"I agree, 100%. Seriously, why do you think they're so popular—the reality shows, I mean."

He blew out air through pursed lips. "I think it depends on the show. The talent competitions—singing, cooking, and the like—we like the idea that any of us could be 'discovered' if we wanted to join in. The others, like this camping thing—it's people behaving badly, and I believe we all like to watch someone acting worse than us. That means we're not so bad. That's my expert opinion. Of course, we've already seen that they do what they can to encourage drama. If everybody played nice and followed instructions, there wouldn't be anything to watch."

Frannie nodded but screwed up her face. "So you think they planned moving this thing to the tent area all along? Get people comfortable in the fancy motor homes and then yanking them out of that comfort zone?"

"Could be. Where did you go on your long walk?"

Frannie grinned. "Down that path to the tent area."

He perked up. "What's going on over there?"

She told him about the wannabe fire builder, and the general angry looks around the area.

"You are giving fire-building instructions?"

"Hey, I've listened to you and Larry go on about it for years. I can not only talk the talk, but walk the walk, too."

Mickey laughed but made no further comment.

Rob came over from his camper with a steaming mug of coffee.

"Gourmet breakfast, Frannie?"

She looked down at the dregs of her bowl of cereal. "Hey, I put bananas on it."

The next hour was consumed by the appearance of the other members of their group and making plans for the day. There was little activity over in the rental RVs; the few people they saw didn't look very happy.

"Does anyone have supper plans?" Mickey asked.

Frannie shook her head. "We look to you for leadership in the food department. Otherwise, we just flounder around."

"Flounder? Is that a seafood joke? Okay, here's a suggestion. One of the most popular local dishes is pasties, and there's a joint on the way to the Point that specializes in them. How about it we break open our wallets and stop there for supper on our way back?"

"What's a pasty?" Rob asked.

"Sort of a meat pie in a crust. We have to try them while we're here."

Donna nodded. "Sounds good to me."

Mickey had all of the information on the glass-bottom boat rides and, after everyone had breakfasted, organized the group in the Shoemaker and Nowak trucks. They headed to the Lake Superior shore.

Frannie gazed out at the passing forest. A few low wooden buildings appeared from time to time, nestled in the trees, but the green dominated. "So different from Iowa."

"You mean cornfields and pine trees don't look the same?" Larry asked.

"Oh, hush."

THE NEXT SCHEDULED BOAT RIDE was a three hour wait, so they decided to take in the Great Lakes Shipwreck Museum nearby. The area included a lighthouse attached to an old two-story home and several red-roofed, white clapboard buildings.

"Hey, there's a film about the *Edmund Fitzgerald* that starts in ten minutes." Mickey pointed at the first house.

"Sounds good," Rob said, "except that now that song is going to run through my head the rest of the day."

After the film, they trooped over to the museum. The numerous shipwrecks in the nearby area were memorialized by displays of a select few, including the *Edmund Fitzgerald*.

Rob pointed at the display of the *Samuel Mather*, sunk in 1891. "Most of these wrecks were collisions. That one got hit by the *Brazil* in fog."

"There were more wrecks here than any part of the lake," Mickey said.

They examined the other displays, mesmerized by the stories of the life-saving attempts, and then stood for a while at the bell of the *Fitzgerald*. Frannie said, "So this is the bell they brought up and replaced with the one with all of the names of the crew that were lost?"

Jane Ann nodded. "The one they talked about in the film. What a sad story."

They went next to the lighthouse keeper's home and lighthouse. The house had been restored and furnished to give visitors an idea of everyday life on the Point in the early 1900s.

"What a lonesome existence," Donna mused.

Larry examined the list of keepers. "That's probably why they didn't last very long—especially in the early years."

Mickey rubbed his hands together. "Who's up for climbing the light house?" He looked pointedly at Frannie.

She looked out the window at the cylindrical shaft braced on all sides by steel framework tapering up to the top. "The steps are inside that tube?"

"Yup."

"I'll try it—but I'm not going out on that deck." She pointed up to the outdoor gallery surrounding the room below the light.

Everyone else was game so they filed through the walkway. The circular metal stairs were enclosed, and their steps echoed through the shaft.

"Almost there?" Frannie called ahead to the leaders. She really needed to get in shape.

"Hang in there," came back. Well, that wasn't helpful. But she made it. They emerged through a hole in the floor of a small enclosed room. Above them was the base of the light.

Mickey, ever their tour guide, pointed up. "There has been a light on there since 1849. It's considered the most important light on Superior. It's only been off one night in all that time."

He paused, waiting for the inevitable question.

"Well?" Rob was the patsy. "When was that?"

"The night the *Fitzgerald* sank. Some kind of power failure. All of their systems went down." He turned for dramatic effect and stepped through the open door onto the gallery that circled the room. The rest followed, except Frannie who stayed inside the door.

"I'll just look from here."

The view was spectacular, especially with the cobalt blue sky. The deeper blue of Superior stretched as far as they could see. The crisp white buildings with their red roofs stood out below them like sugar cubes on a piece of astroturf.

"Wow! Gorgeous!" she said.

Larry grinned back at her. "Even better out here."

"I can see just fine, thank you."

After several minutes, Mickey began herding them all back to the door. "If we're going to make our boat, we gotta get going."

They clambered back down the echoing stairs and headed for their trucks.

CHAPTER SEVEN
WEDNESDAY AFTERNOON

AT THE DOCK for the glass-bottom cruises, they were directed to one of the green and white excursion boats. Inside, benches lined the walls under the windows. Two underwater viewing windows sat parallel in the center of the floor, each with its own white railing. Only a few other people, mostly senior citizens, sat on the benches. One young woman with a halo of red curls caught Frannie's eye. She nudged Larry.

"Isn't that the woman from the canoe yesterday?"

Larry squinted. "I think so. She doesn't seem to recognize us, though."

"I'm not surprised. Who would in those circumstances?"

An open deck at the rear allowed passengers to sit outside to view the scenery if they wished. Frannie's group took seats inside on one side of a viewing window.

Mickey had informed them earlier that besides the two shipwrecks that they would view, the boat would cruise the part of the lakeshore known as the Pictured Rocks, famous for the varieties of colors and arches.

The beautiful day accentuated the imposing formations of the cliffs, striated and streaked with color. The Battleship Rocks reminded Frannie of World War II era photos she had seen of Pearl Harbor. Formations such as the Lover's Leap and the Grand Portal featured natural arches. The cliff faces resembled slabs of finely layered cakes dripping with carmel, chocolate, and white frosting. Perhaps a dab of licorice here and there.

Frannie couldn't stop snapping pictures. Each vista seemed more stunning than the last. Others on their boat had their cameras and phones out as well. Wives tugged at their husbands' sleeves to point out the Indian Head or the Flower Vase. The cliffs were topped by pines and fall foliage and lapped on the bottom by the lazy waves of the lake.

"This is just awesome, Mick. Good job on this choice."

"Thanks. I would bow but I don't want to fall through that glass." They looked down just as a school of fish darted beneath them.

Jane Ann sighed and leaned back against the bench. "There's too much to see."

"You're so right," Rob said. "Look behind you—there's a freighter out there."

Donna whirled around. "Omigosh! This is better than the celebrities!" Jane Ann and Frannie exchanged eye rolls, a common transaction when Donna was around.

"When do we see the shipwrecks?" Donna turned back and grabbed Mickey's arm.

53

"I think it's toward the end."

"Great! I can't wait."

Mickey rubbed his arm. "It is a pretty spectacular choice, if I do say so myself."

They continued to ooh and aah over each turn in the cliffs, trading comments with the other passengers.

The tour guide, a young woman in khakis and a navy polo shirt had kept up a running commentary on the names of the formations and the causes of the colors that gave the cliffs their name. She finally said into her mike, "We're coming up on the first shipwreck, so you'll want to watch the viewing window. This one is the *Herman Hettler* that went down in 1926, fortunately with no loss of life." She went on to explain that due to a faulty compass reading, the ship had gone aground and over the next couple of days, storms battered it to pieces. The wreckage was now strewn across the lake bottom.

The passengers all got up and stood around the viewing windows. Gradually parts of the relic came into view.

"There's the anchor," Rob said, pointing. "Kind of hard to recognize some of the stuff."

The blue-green of the water softened the outlines of objects and gave the window a dream-like quality.

An older man at the other window, suddenly shouted, "There's a toilet! And a bathtub!"

The tour guide smiled. "Yes, that's the Captain's commode and his tub. The other wreck that we will see is more intact, the *Bermuda*. Part of the hull of the *Hettler*

54

was dynamited by the Coast Guard because it blocked navigation. An interesting side fact is that the *Hettler* was loaded with table salt."

"Is that why they call sailors 'salts'?" Mickey asked, with his usual impish grin. It earned him a few chuckles and even more groans.

The boat entered a channel leading to a small harbor and the passengers returned to their seats. The guide pointed out the Grand Island East Channel Lighthouse.

Frannie smiled. "It almost looks like the Little Brown Church in Nashua, Iowa, except for the light on the steeple."

"And without the brown paint," Mickey said.

The lighthouse did resemble an old weathered church with a square steeple in front. The gray cedar siding and stone foundation contrasted with the deep green pines and amber and burgundy foliage surrounding it. Cameras and phones blossomed again among the passengers.

The guide continued. "It's privately owned and was restored with private funds and community help."

The excursion boat rounded the southern tip of the island and slowed. "We are just about over the *Bermuda* so watch the viewing windows." They all stood again and lined the railings. This time the boat shape was clearly discernible. "She was 136 feet long, filled with iron ore, and sunk in 1870."

"Wow!" Jane Ann said. "Almost one hundred and fifty years ago."

They peered down at the glass as the wreck was exposed to their view a section at a time, scrolling under them like a slow motion movie. The nebulous edges of the planks and the soft colors were mesmerizing.

Until the face came into view.

Gasps and muted screams erupted from both groups of watchers.

"What is it?" asked the guide, interested but not alarmed.

"A person — a body!"

"No." A harsh laugh from one of the men. "It's staged, a dummy — just to give us all a fright."

The guide looked puzzled, moved over to the window next to Frannie, and stared down. A face with softened features and silvery hair floating in a halo around it stared up at them. "Oh, my God!" She turned to the pilot. "Captain Keltz! Can you stop the boat? It looks like a drowning! Too late for rescue, I think though." She looked at the man who thought it was a trick. "This is not staged. It's no joke."

Frannie tugged Larry's sleeve. "It's the — "

"Producer. I know. Cliff Remboski."

The captain stopped the boat and called the local rescue team with the Sheriff's department. "Tell them to bring divers," Frannie heard him say.

People milled around the viewing windows, checking to make sure they hadn't been seeing things and then backing off in horror. The volume of voices built as all of the passengers talked at once.

The guide turned to Larry. Frannie noticed the name 'Ashley' embroidered on her shirt. "Did I hear you say that you know him?"

"Just that we met him last night at the campground. He's a TV producer and they're filming a reality show there."

Ashley looked down at the specter in the water. "Really?" She swallowed and shook her head.

Just then, the captain called Ashley over. Frannie heard him say, "I'm going to move away from the wreck to help people calm down. As soon as the Guard and the local crews arrive, we'll head back. See if you can get people seated again."

Ashley nodded and picked up her microphone. She had lost much of the color in her face and pushed strands of long brown hair back from her eyes. "Folks! Folks, please! We would like you to sit down again. The Coast Guard has been called, and we need to move away from the site, so that they will be able to perform a rescue—I mean, a recovery."

Her choice of words had a more quieting effect, and people took their seats, talking quietly to their spouses or friends. The pilot moved the boat a short distance away. Ashley spoke to him in a low voice and pointed at Larry. He responded and she returned to Larry.

"Captain Keltz is sure the authorities will want to talk to you when we dock, so can you wait after the other passengers get off?"

"Certainly."

Frannie sat in shock. Several times, her group had been caught up in deaths on previous camping trips. Other campers she knew *never* had this kind of thing happen. Why was it happening again?

Soon a sheriff's boat pulled up next to the excursion boat. The pilot, Captain Keltz, spoke into a mike and pointed to the area where the body was. They exchanged a few more words and Keltz pulled the excursion boat away, making a wide U-turn and heading back to the boat dock near the point. A diver on the stern of the rescue boat was preparing to go into the water.

The grisly discovery took the bright edge off the afternoon, and the ride back was quiet. Conversations were carried out in low tones, and people stared out the windows but not really seeing the vividly-colored cliffs and the unique formations. It seemed to take forever, but eventually they pulled in at the dock. The passengers filed off in an orderly manner. Captain Keltz and Ashley led them to the company offices where two desk clerks took contact information from everyone.

The captain approached Larry. "Did you say you are camping in the area?"

Larry nodded. "We're at the campground at Ojibway Falls."

"Okay. If you've given your contact information to Faye or Dorothy, you can go back there. It will be a while before the authorities are ready to talk to people." He looked apologetic. "It will take some time to process the scene and notify family."

"Process the scene?" Frannie said. "You don't think he just drowned?"

"Um, that's not for me to say. So you are going back to the campground now?"

The others were still ruminating on Captain Keltz's answer, so Mickey said "We were going to stop for supper, but we could just get take-out?" He looked around the group.

"Yeah."

"Sure."

"Fine with me."

They trooped back to the trucks.

"Cliff seemed like a pretty nice guy—certainly more reasonable than his assistant," Frannie said. "If it wasn't an accidental drowning, who would want to kill him?"

Larry unlocked his truck. "We only spoke to him for about fifteen minutes last night. Pretty hard to judge his character from that."

Frannie pulled herself up into the backseat so that Mickey could ride in front and give directions. Jane Ann was riding with the Nowaks.

"I suppose. I guess we *have* witnessed him in two different altercations."

"Two?" Larry started the truck and backed out. "Yesterday when we were on the hike, we saw him arguing with that country singer. When else?"

"This morning before you got your lazy butt out of bed," Mickey said. "Frannie and I saw him arguing with another guy over by their rental RVs. Turn left up here at this next corner."

"Let me remind you that we don't know that it *wasn't* an accident."

"And let me remind you that Frannie's here. It's always murder when she's around."

Frannie piped up from the back seat. "Mickey, stop saying that, or I'm going to wring your neck!"

Mickey shrugged and looked at Larry. "See what I mean? Straight through that stoplight, and this place should be on the right in the next block."

Larry laughed and then tried to counter it with "Sorry, dear." He parked in front of the pasty shop. "Everyone going in?"

Frannie opened her door. "I certainly don't trust either of you to order for me."

"Aw, see Mick? You hurt her feelings."

"You guys are mean. You haven't changed since junior high."

"You didn't know us in junior high," Mickey said as he held the door to the shop for her.

"Thank God. For your information, I will not get involved in this murder in any way."

The clerk behind the counter looked up in alarm at her last comment.

"We don't know it's a murder," Larry mumbled, and then spoke up to the clerk. "You have pasties for take-out?"

"Sure do. What can I help you with?" Very friendly, although he continued to cast wary glances at Frannie.

Rob, Donna, and Jane followed them in. They perused the menu posted on the wall and asked questions about the offerings. Finally, they made their choices.

"I'll have the veggie," Jane Ann said.

Frannie nodded. "Me too."

Larry and Rob ordered the beef, and Mickey and Donna opted for the pork. While they waited, they examined the tee shirts and coffee mugs for sale on one side of the shop. Frannie held up a white mug with an outline map of Michigan to the clerk . The Upper Peninsula was labeled 'Yoopers' and Lower Michigan was labeled 'Trolls.'

"I know what a Yooper is. What's a troll?"

He grinned. "The people who live below The Bridge."

"Ohhh. The Mackinac Bridge?"

"Yup. Around here, that is *The* Bridge."

Mickey added a Green Bay Packers shirt to his bill.

The clerk said, "I'll throw in a couple of tubs of gravy with your order. Do you want any coleslaw?"

They all declined; he figured up their bills and handed them several sacks. As they got back in the truck, Mickey said with a smirk, "I bet he's writing down our plate number, after your murder comment, Frannie."

Frannie sighed and gave up trying to defend herself.

On the way back to the park, Mickey pulled out his phone.

"Oooh," he said, after studying it a few moments.

"What?" Larry asked.

"Looks like we might be getting some more weather tonight or tomorrow. A front coming in. Worst part is, temps could drop below freezing."

"That's not good. We'd better keep an eye on it." Larry turned the truck into the campground. They waved at the woman in the check-in shack and continued back to their sites.

CHAPTER EIGHT
WEDNESDAY EVENING

THEY PARKED AND EMERGED from the trucks. It was only five o'clock and still pleasant enough to eat outside. Mickey offered to rewarm the pasties and gravy in his oven. Donna and Jane Ann set the table, Frannie took Cuba for a short walk, and Larry and Rob started a fire. There was no activity in the rental encampment.

As they settled around the table, Madelyn Mays came by. "Don't let me interrupt, but just wanted to check how your day was. Did you get to do the shipwreck cruise?"

They looked at each other, not sure how much they were or weren't supposed to say.

"Yeah, we did," Frannie said. "A beautiful cruise. I think I took hundreds of pictures."

"Good. It's been pretty quiet here. Except that assistant producer, Brandee Tudor, has been driving me crazy. Apparently, the producer hasn't shown up all day, and she seems to think I know where he is." She shook her head in frustration.

Looks were exchanged again, and this time Madelyn caught them. "What? Have you seen him?"

"Actually, yes, we have," Larry said. He described the events of the afternoon.

Madelyn sucked in a deep breath. "He's dead?"

They all nodded.

"Oh, wow. I have no idea what this will do to this whole project, but I guess it's up to the rangers and the park manager to handle it. Ms. Tudor is going to go ballistic when she hears the news." She paused a moment. "That sounds really hard-hearted, and I don't mean it that way. They'll probably just send everyone home. I wonder if he had family. How did it happen? Do they know why he was out there?"

Larry shook his head. "We don't know anything else. I'm sure the authorities will be here soon."

"Oh-oh, Madelyn. Here comes your little friend." Mickey nodded in the direction of the rental RVs.

Ms. Red Cap—actually today in a dark green ball cap—marched toward them, clipboard in hand. She ignored the rest of the group and got in Madelyn's face.

"Mrs. Mays. This has gone on long enough. I think something has happened to Cliff. How do I get in touch with the Park officials? Or should I just call 911?"

Larry said, "Ms. Tudor, that isn't going to be necessary. You are right—something did happen to Mr. Remboski." He got up from the table while Brandee Tudor just stared at him. He pointed toward the campground entrance. "The sheriff is coming now, and I'll just flag him down."

Since the road was one-way, every vehicle headed for the rental RV sites had to pass the Shoemakers' group first. While they waited, Frannie noticed that the temperature seemed to be dropping and the sky was darker, not only because of the coming night.

Larry stepped out to the road to stop the sheriff's cruiser. The sheriff lowered the window and Larry introduced himself, explaining that they had been present when the body was discovered. The sheriff stepped out of his car and walked toward the waiting group.

"This is Sheriff Elliot." Larry indicated the production assistant. "Sheriff, this is Brandee Tudor. She was Mr. Remboski's assistant."

Brandee backed up, her eyes wide. "Was? *Was*? What's going on? Have I been fired and no one even told me?" She threw her clipboard to the ground and began to walk away.

Larry started to go after her, but the sheriff held up his hand. "Ms. Tudor! I'm afraid Mr. Rembowski has met with tragedy."

She turned slowly, eyes now ready to pop. "Wh-hat?"

"Mr. Remboski was found dead today in the lake."

She dropped down on the picnic bench. It began to rain, but she didn't seem to notice.

"Dead?"

Frannie ducked in the camper and put out their awning. "Here, everyone come under here, and at least stay dry."

Jane Ann and Donna grabbed the food off the table and took it inside. They all moved under the awning, but it was crowded. Larry indicated the door to the trailer.

"Would you like to go inside?"

The sheriff shook his head. "This won't take long. I need to get over and talk to the others, too."

Larry moved a lawn chair to a dry spot for Brandee. She didn't look like she could stand.

Sheriff Elliot put his hands on his hips and faced her. "Can you tell me when was the last time you saw him?"

"Uh," she looked down at her hands and then back at the sheriff. "Last night, I guess."

The sheriff scanned the rest of the group. "Anyone else see him since then?" The patter of the rain on the awning increased, almost like a drumroll. Frannie and Mickey raised their hands tentatively.

Mickey said, "This morning, he was outside over there arguing kind of loudly with another man." He indicated the loop where the rental RVs stood.

The sheriff raised his eyebrows. "Did you know this other man?" Frannie and Mickey both shook their heads.

"We hadn't seen him before," Frannie said.

"What did he look like?"

"Grey sweatshirt," Mickey said.

"Dark windbreaker or jacket. Maybe navy or dark green," Frannie said at the same time.

Larry put his hand to his forehead. "C'mon you guys. Height? Fat or skinny? Hair color?"

Mickey said to the sheriff, "Retired cop."

Sheriff Elliot drew up in surprise. "The man Remboski was arguing with?"

"No, I mean Larry is. Sorry. Um, the guy was definitely shorter than Rembowski. A little on the heavy side."

Frannie nodded in agreement. "Didn't he have kind of a pony tail?" she asked Mickey.

He shrugged. "Too far to see. But definitely light hair, wouldn't you say?"

"Yeah, not dark anyway."

The sheriff looked exasperated, but just sighed. Larry stepped in. "Sheriff, yesterday we were on a hike around the island in the river, and we also saw Remboski arguing with another man then. They were on the other side of the falls on the deck, and we couldn't hear anything, but it obviously wasn't friendly. I think the other guy's name is Cooper Wainwright."

"The country singer?"

Brandee Tudor had recovered enough to respond. "Yes, Sheriff. The pilot we're shooting is called *Celebrity Campout.*"

"Sorry. I didn't know he was still alive. Wainwright, I mean. Do you know what they might have been arguing about?"

She shifted in her chair. "Well, Cliff had kind of a thing for Coop's ex-wife."

"Tassi Ketchum?" Frannie asked.

"Yeah."

"Okay." Sheriff Elliot peered out at the persistent rain. "Where are the rest of the people in this — show?" He looked back at Brandee.

"They're in the tent area."

The sheriff cocked his head and looked at her in wonder. "You have all of those big motor homes over there, and the people in your show are in *tents*?"

She sighed. More dealings with rubes. "It's a long story and has nothing to do with Cliff's death." She looked up at him. "You haven't said whether it was an accident or not."

"What makes you think it was *not* an accident?"

"Because you are asking about arguments that he had. What would that have to do with an accident?" She definitely had regained her composure.

"Would you just show me where these tents are?"

Brandee got up. "If you'll give me a ride. I'm not walking in this."

"Certainly." He bowed and swept his arm toward his cruiser. Brandy pulled her jacket over her head and ran for the passenger side.

"You'll be here?" He looked at the campers.

"All evening," Mickey said.

The sheriff jogged to his car.

They all stood around a moment. Then Larry said, "Let's go inside."

Madelyn Mays hung back. "I should probably be going."

"Not in this." Rob nodded toward the worsening rain. "Come in and we'll see if it lets up. If not we'll loan you an umbrella."

Frannie turned on the electric fireplace/space heater and started shuffling plates through the microwave.

"Madelyn, we have plenty if you would like some."

The host looked up from petting Cuba. "Thank you, no — we just finished supper before I came over. So, what do you guys think? It sounds like it wasn't an accident or natural causes."

Larry continued to be noncommittal. "Maybe when he comes back, we'll find out."

Frannie swallowed a big bite of veggie pasty. "These are really good. So what do you suppose they'll do about the filming?"

"Don't know. Somebody put up a lot of money, I imagine. Maybe Brandee will take over," Madelyn said.

Frannie said, not to anyone in particular, "Why would Brandee think the sheriff would be coming to tell her she was fired?" Several shrugged, but no one had any ideas.

Mickey grimaced. "Poor celebrities."

"Right." She got up. "Sounds like the rain is letting up. I'd better get back. My husband will think I drowned." She caught herself. "Oh! Sorry."

They said goodbye and she left.

Rob and Jane Ann took care of the clean up and they all settled back with their beverages.

"Could be a long wait for the sheriff to come back if he has to interview all of those people," Frannie said. "No TV reception, but we've got a couple of movies. Or we could play a game."

"I'm not up for a game. I need more distraction. What are your movies?" Donna said.

Frannie opened the cupboard behind the TV and pulled out several DVDs. "Um, *Psycho*, *Girl on the Train*, *Saving Private Ryan*…here's a classic: *The Long, Long Trailer*."

"The old Lucille Ball one?" Mickey asked. "That sounds good. The others are too dark for the day we've had."

Donna wagged her head. "I agree."

Frannie clicked on the TV and put the disc in. Larry fiddled with the remote, grumbling. "I don't know why you need over fifty buttons to run a DVD player."

They were soon engrossed in the silly tale of a young couple buying their first trailer. It was a relief to escape the darkness around them.

"Hey, Jane Ann!" Mickey said. "You need to dress better for camping. Look at that—heels, pearls, dress, hat…"

"I'll be glad to, as soon as you wear a suit and tie," she answered. "And a hat like that, except you'd look like a gangster."

The distraction of the movie was enough that they didn't notice the rain getting harder, until Rob sat up with alarm. "Is that ice?"

Larry hit the mute button on the remote. Sure enough, the pelting on the roof had a more distinct sound than just the patter of the rain. Mickey pulled out his phone to check the radar.

"Oh, man—not looking good." He held the phone up so the others could see the large blob of pink and purple.

"Mick, I thought you told us just a chance of *light* rain tomorrow. You didn't mention this," Rob said.

"Hey, I can't be perfect all of the time."

Larry jumped up from his chair.

"What is it?" Frannie said in alarm.

"The awning is still out." He rushed to the door and tried to push it open. "Aggh! It's sagging—there must be so much ice on it! I'll have to get it off before I can close it." He grabbed his coat and the broom hanging on a wall hook.

Everyone was up, looking for coats and shoes and bumping into each other. Spacious in a camper is not like spacious in a house.

Larry had forced the door open far enough to squeeze outside. He was using the broom to jab the awning in places to break up the ice on top. Chunks slid off and crashed to the ground—at first, small pieces and then larger ones. Frannie got a sponge mop out of a utility closet and joined him. The others squeezed outside to check their own units, slipping and sliding on the ice-crusted grass.

As Frannie worked on one end of the awning while Larry tried to clear the other, she heard Mickey yell, "Our door's frozen shut!"

Frannie never broke her pace but responded. "There's a hair dryer in our bathroom under the sink."

Jane Ann skated back across the grass. As she went up the steps through the partially open door, she called out, "Extension cord?"

"In the footstool."

By the time Mickey got the cord plugged into his outdoor outlet and started to work on his door, Larry yelled to Frannie, "I think that's most of it. I'm going to try and close it before it gets covered again." He clambered up the steps and pushed the button just inside the door. The awning began to slowly roll up until it got about half-way and stopped. They went to work again on the top half. Rob appeared with a broom to help.

"You able to get in your camper okay?" Larry asked him. Jab. Jab. Jab.

"Yeah." Jab. Jab. "Our door faces the other way."

"Good. Frannie, try to finish closing it."

She went up the steps and hit the button. It started up again and began to roll. A chunk of ice fell off and hit Rob in the shoulder.

"Hope you're insured, Shoemaker!" he said, brushing it off with a grin. The awning stopped with about six inches to go.

Jane Ann returned with the hair dryer, cord, and a report of success. They glanced over to see Mickey standing on his steps in triumph in front of his open door.

They worked on the last section and finally succeeded in getting the awning closed. Rob loped off toward his own trailer.

Inside, Larry got an old towel out of the cupboard to dry his face. Frannie came up behind him and hugged him. "We're too old for this, honey. We need a more restful hobby."

He turned and smiled. "You are so right. How about a glass of wine and we'll finish the movie?"

Her response was interrupted by pounding on the door. "Ferraro, I bet," Larry said. He went to open the door, prepared with an insult. The sheriff stood at the bottom of the steps looking up at him.

"We need help," the sheriff said.

•

CHAPTER NINE
WEDNESDAY NIGHT

LARRY INSISTED THAT Sheriff Elliot come in, since the icy rain still pelted the area. He stood just inside the door wiping his face with his hand. Frannie handed him a towel.

"Thanks. We've got a mess over there in that tent area. Several people were hurt from falling branches and the tents are collapsing with the ice. We need to get them back to those motor homes, but some of them might have to be carried out. I don't know how many injuries we've got."

Larry already had his coat back on and was texting Mickey and Rob. Frannie pulled a couple of extra blankets out of the closet.

"My sister's a nurse," Larry told Sheriff Elliot as they followed him out. The doors on the Shoemaker truck were frozen shut.

"Ride with me," the sheriff said. "What about your friends?"

In answer, Rob's truck roared to life and his headlights came on. "Mickey and Jane Ann can ride with him," Larry said.

The sheriff took off with Larry in the front and Frannie in the back, not exactly under the campground speed limit. At the other side of the loop, he pulled to the side by the path and they got out. As they hurried down the path, heads ducked to keep the rain off their faces, the sheriff continued his report.

"I was interviewing people when branches started to fall. The hosts got there with the golf cart, and we can get the most seriously injured out that way. I've called for ambulances, but with this ice, who knows how long it will take them. My deputies are all tied up with a couple of bad accidents over on the highway. What a night!"

The Ferraros and the Nowaks came up behind them. Larry relayed the situation to them.

When they reached the tent camp, an eerie scene greeted them. The only light came from the golf cart headlights and a battery powered lantern sitting cockeyed on a picnic table. The meager beams picked out the crystal ice drops outlining tent poles and trees. Madelyn Mays and her husband were trying to get a man into the passenger seat of the golf cart. His leg was at an awkward angle, and he screamed in pain. Jane Ann rushed over to see what she could do.

Other people, including Brandee Tudor, tried to lift a huge branch off a tent. A woman and man sat hugging each other on a picnic bench.

Frannie turned to the sheriff. "What do you want us to do first?"

He shook his head. "Talk to Mrs. Mays. She's been here since the ice started."

They trudged over to the golf cart. Frannie could already feel the cold damp seeping through the back of her coat and her toes were freezing. The ice continued to pelt their faces. And these poor people had been out in this an hour or more?

"Madelyn! How can we help?"

Madelyn turned. "Oh, thank goodness. Please check all of the tents and make sure we don't miss anyone. Then help anyone who can walk, get out to those motor homes. Sheriff Elliot said he doesn't know how soon an ambulance can get here."

Larry took charge of the group. "Frannie and I will check the tents on this side. Rob, you, Donna, and Mickey take the other side."

They split up and the Shoemakers started with the nearest tent. It was still standing and was empty. The next one was partially down and someone was moving under the collapsed side.

Larry ducked his head inside. "Anyone here?"

A weak whimper came from the pile of canvas. Larry crawled in and came out with a black shaking mass.

"What is it?" Frannie asked around her chattering teeth.

"A dog." He handed the small shivering creature to Frannie. It burrowed into her chest and looked up at her with huge black eyes.

"Oh my gosh." She unzipped her coat with one hand and arranged the dog underneath next to the warmth of her body.

Larry had already moved on to the next tent. It was completely collapsed and so flat that it seemed highly unlikely that anyone could be in it, but he checked anyway.

"No one." They moved on.

The next tent was the one crushed by the large branch. Brandee and two others had just succeeded in getting the branch off to the side. Someone inside called for help. The desperate voice sounded like a man. Frannie couldn't do much while hanging on to the dog, but Larry and Brandee unzipped the flap and laid it open. An older man lay on his back, holding his left arm with his right.

Brandee leaned over him. "Tommy! We're here. Is your arm the only problem? Can you walk? We need to get you somewhere warm and dry."

He opened his eyes. "I think—my legs are okay." Deep breath. "But I don't think I can get up." He erupted in a dry laugh. "Poetic justice, I guess."

Brandee looked up at Frannie and Larry. "He's done some of those health alert 'I can't get up' ads." She turned back to Tommy. "We can help you sit up first, and then this nice man and I will get you to your feet." Obviously, Brandee could be pleasant when she needed help.

"Thanks."

77

Larry pulled the tent away from him, and together, they managed to get Tommy sitting. He moaned.

Larry said, "Okay, put your good arm around my neck, and I'll get you by the waist. Then we'll try and stand." Larry crouched beside the injured man. Brandee got on the other side and also put her arm around the man's waist.

"On three," Larry said. "One, two — three!"

The man yelped, but they managed to get him to his feet. Fortunately he was of very small stature. Once he was standing, he used his right arm again to support his left.

"What do you think, Tommy? Can you walk back to the RVs? Otherwise we can get you a ride in the golf cart, but you might have to wait a bit," Brandee said.

He nodded. "I think I can walk."

Frannie said, "I can't be of much help and hang on to this dog. Why don't I walk him back, find someone to take the dog, and come back."

"Good idea," Larry said.

Frannie led the man toward the path. "I'm Frannie Shoemaker, by the way."

"Are you on the production staff?"

"The what? Oh, no, we're just staying in the campground."

He smiled a little. "You do this for fun?"

"We do. Of course, some times are more fun than others. Are you Tommy Pratt?"

He looked surprised. "Do you remember me? You look too young."

Frannie laughed. "You flatter me. I watched your show as a kid."

"That's long past. Oof!" He stumbled a little, and Frannie caught him by his good arm.

"Careful—you don't need any more injuries." She concentrated her flashlight beam on the ground right in front of them.

"You are so right. Anyway, now I'm lucky to get a few commercials, a bit part here and there, and stupid projects like this one."

"So, if I may ask, what is the goal of this show?"

"To make us all look like fools."

She smiled. "Seriously, what are you supposed to accomplish?"

He shrugged. "There's all kinds of rules. The winner is supposed to get a chance to co-host on an RV makeover show. There were points for setting up a tent and starting a fire. And all of the tents had parts missing —stakes or poles—to make it more of a challenge."

"Wait up!" came a call from behind them. They stopped and turned around. Tassi Ketchum, minus the architecturally designed hairdo, hobbled toward them, tears or rain streaming down her face. Dark streaks on her face appeared to be bruises until Frannie realized it was makeup smudged by the rain. She clutched a sodden-looking blanket around her shoulders.

"Tommy, did you hear about Cliff? He's dead." Now she was sobbing.

"What? Where did you hear that?"

"The sheriff came when the storm started. You were asleep, I think." She used the wet blanket to wipe her face.

"It's true," Frannie said. "We were on the glass-bottom cruise when he was found in the water."

Tassi whirled toward her as if she was seeing her for the first time. "Who are you?" Then she softened. "Oh, you helped me with the fire this morning."

Tommy muttered, "You're not supposed to get outside help." He was slowing down and clutching his arm.

"I don't care. I just want this over."

They reached the end of the path. Frannie said, "You both need to get inside, dry off, and get warmed up. Do you know if any of the RVs are open?"

They shook their heads. Several people had already walked out of the tent area. They had to be somewhere. Lights glowed from one of the motor homes.

"Let's try that one."

The door was unlocked. Frannie held the door for Tommy and Brandee, and then followed them in. Four or five people sat around wrapped in blankets, and everyone talked at once. Frannie pulled the dog out from under her coat and set it on the floor. He immediately ran to a woman at the dinette, jumped in her lap, and began licking her face.

"Oh, Grizzly!" The woman looked at Frannie. "Where did you find him?"

"In a collapsed tent. I need to get back and see who else needs help." She turned to Tassi. "You'll keep an eye on Tommy until an ambulance gets here? His arm may be broken." Tassi nodded, and Frannie headed back out the door.

As she picked her way down the path, her mind looped through a tangle of thoughts. Cliff Remboski's death had been pushed into the background for the time being by subsequent events. If it was murder, Frannie would have thought Brandee Tudor would be the more likely candidate as a victim, as annoying and abrasive as she could be. But it was Cliff they had seen arguing with two different men. One was Cooper Wainwright, and his ex-wife seemed especially broken up by Cliff's death. Had there been something there? On the other hand, lots of people got involved in arguments, and it rarely resulted in murder.

She came back to earth as she met Mickey helping two women up the path. He babbled as fast as a telemarketer, and their eyes appeared glazed.

"There's at least one of those RVs open," Frannie told him as she passed.

"Thanks!"

She had just reached the tent area when she heard the golf cart putt up behind her. The icy rain was finally letting up and a thin moon even peered from the clouds.

Madelyn pulled along side her. Chet was not in the cart. "The ambulance was just arriving as I left."

Frannie glanced back and could see the scarlet flash of the lights through the trees. "Good. Are there many serious injuries?"

"I think a broken leg and a possible concussion. Who knows how many will be sick from being out in this mess." She glanced up and noticed the moon. "Maybe it's finally done."

"Tommy Pratt might have a broken arm."

Madelyn sighed. "Who knew this would turn into such a fiasco?"

They looked around the site. Larry and Chet were talking to the sheriff. Jane Ann was packing up a first aid kit and Donna and Rob were rechecking the fallen tents. On the edge of the encampment, a young man with a huge camera on his shoulder documented the turmoil. Frannie shook her head, got in the golf cart with Madelyn, and they bumped over to their husbands.

Larry hugged Frannie. "You look like a wet dog."

"Thank you." But she grinned. "Sheriff, are you still wanting to interview us more?"

He took off his hat and mopped his forehead. "In the morning. We're not going to solve any murders tonight. I can't thank you enough for your help here."

Chet Mays said, "I'll second that."

"Go find somewhere warm and get some sleep," Sheriff Elliot added.

Jane Ann brought the first aid kit to the sheriff, and Rob and Donna joined them.

"Do you need a ride back to your campers?" the sheriff asked.

Rob shook his head. "We can all get in my truck for that short distance."

"I'll see you in the morning then."

Madelyn told Donna and Jane Ann to hop in the back of the cart, and sped off back to the road. They jeered at Rob and Larry who had to walk behind. Rob just laughed at them.

As Madelyn let them out at the truck, Donna said, "I know why Rob was laughing. He has the keys, and the truck's locked."

Sure, enough, Mickey leaned against the truck, arms crossed. "Locked," was all he said.

While they waited, they checked out the campground. The ambulance had gone again. Brandee was unlocking the other RVs, and people shrouded in blankets rushed to get into them.

Larry and Rob emerged from the path, ambling without a care in the world and laughing.

"Hurry up," Donna called, stamping her feet to warm them up. Rob waved the keys in the air.

"You could have walked and let me ride," he said as he unlocked the truck and they piled in. After a very short ride, they wasted no time getting back to their own units.

"Do you want to watch the rest of the movie?" Larry said to Frannie with a grin.

"You go ahead if you want. I'm going to bed."

"Just kidding. I'm ready to fold."

She brushed her teeth, hurried into her flannel pajamas and crawled under the thick comforter. Larry was soon beside her.

"Larry," she said, before giving in to heavy eyelids, "did you notice that the sheriff said we weren't going to solve any *murders* tonight?"

"Yup. Go to sleep."

CHAPTER TEN
THURSDAY MORNING

DOWNED BRANCHES WERE the only sign the next morning of the havoc created the night before. The sun warmed the campground nicely, in the process destroying all of the diamond drops created by the ice. Frannie wasn't sorry about that, as she and Cuba sat on a bench overlooking the river.

She recalled the cameraman lurking around the edges of the chaos. A little real 'reality' for a change? And the sheriff used the word 'murder' to describe Cliff's death. Was this an internal thing—a killer within the cast or staff? But why would someone be upset enough to murder the producer? Or was it a random killing? And where? She and Mickey had seen Cliff Rembowski in the campground early that morning. A few hours later he was dead in Lake Superior miles away. Brandee's reaction to the sheriff's appearance was strange too. She was so engrossed in her thoughts that she didn't hear footsteps behind her.

"Here." Her husband came around the bench and handed her a steaming mug of coffee.

She looked up in surprise as she accepted the mug. "You're up early!"

He sat beside her. "Sometimes I get up early."

"The last time was in 1986."

"Bah. Not true."

"Thank you for the coffee anyway."

Larry looked out at the river while warming his hands on his mug. "Beautiful spot. But I bet you're thinking about murder, aren't you?"

She started to deny it, but then said, "Why would you think that?"

"What was the last thing you said last night before you went to sleep?"

"Oh. Yeah. Well, I think the sheriff let it slip. I don't think he meant to say that."

"Probably not."

"What do you think?"

He gazed at her. "Think? I've hardly met any of those people. It's like one of those movies where someone witnesses a murder on a passing train—you know, no context. We were there when they found the body and we heard him arguing with two people. We know *nothing* else about it."

She smiled. "But they always solve those mysteries. I know Miss Marple did."

"And that's why that's called *fiction*."

She sighed. He always worried that she would get involved. Maybe because she usually did.

"Well, anyway—I wonder what they'll do about the pilot now. It occurred to me that someone put up a lot of money to do this. I don't think they'll cancel just because the director was murdered — er, died."

"Maybe not."

"Did you notice that at least one cameraman was still filming last night when we were headed back?"

"So it sounds like they *are* going to go on." He put his arm around her shoulders. "Now let's enjoy this lovely morning, or I'll never get up early again."

MICKEY WAS MAKING PANCAKES when they got back to the campsite. "Oh, ho! You guys just coming home from your date last night?"

Frannie laughed. "Some date! You guys really know how to entertain a girl!"

Jane Ann set a tray with syrup, butter, plates and forks on the table. "Good morning!"

Mickey swung the grill holding his cast iron griddle away from the fire and began scooping pancakes on to a plate. "Well, you're just in time! Grab a plate. Juice and coffee on the table over there."

Larry stopped short and stared. "Wait. *You* made your own coffee?"

Frannie sat down hard on the picnic table bench and said to Jane Ann, "Larry got up early and Mickey made coffee? Is this the end of the world?"

"Could be."

Rob and Donna came around the end of Ferraros' motor home.

"Great day, campers!" Rob said and set a foil-covered plate on the table. It smelled a lot like sausage.

"Certainly better than last night," Larry said. Talk ceased the next few minutes as they forked golden pancakes onto their plates, passed butter, syrup, and sausage. Cuba wandered around the table, following the sausage platter.

"So." Mickey waited for the rest to look at him. "We haven't been to the Upper Falls yet. We can either hike there from the Lower Falls or drive back to the highway and up to the other park entrance. There's some gift shops and a couple of restaurants there, too."

Donna clapped her hands, and her spiky hair vibrated. "Shopping!"

"You know, I *would* like to pick up a new sweatshirt," Jane Ann said.

Frannie agreed. "I could use a little retail therapy. So stressful last night being a hero."

"Girls! Girls!" Mickey pounded his plate with his fork. "We're discussing whether to hike up to the falls or drive."

"*You* mentioned the shops," Frannie said.

"That was just a footnote. You know, like when you get home and someone asks 'Were there any shops around?' and you can say 'Oh yeah, I think Mickey said there were.' Now, the hike to the Upper Falls is four miles beyond the Lower Falls."

Frannie got up and started stacking plates. "Don't forget that Sheriff Elliot said he was coming back this morning."

"Right. But when we're ready to go, I'd be up for a hike," Rob said.

Donna shook her head at him. "What if we have a lot of packages from shopping? We wouldn't want to carry them back four miles."

"Thanks, Ferraro, for bringing up the shops," Rob said. "Drive it is."

Frannie smiled. "Good. I'm not sure if I'd be up for four miles anyway, after last night."

It looked like no one else was either, except Rob.

"Good morning!" called a determined voice. Frannie turned in her chair and was shocked to see Brandee Tudor headed their way with an actual smile on her face.

"I just wanted to thank you people for all of your help last night. What an awful day." She reached the table. "Mind if I sit?"

"Certainly not," Frannie said, trying to adjust to this new Brandee.

"I also want to apologize for my rudeness before. This is a pretty stressful job, and I don't have Cliff's patience." She stopped and her eyes teared up.

"I'm really sorry. He seemed like a nice man."

"Well," Brandee swiped at her eyes, "the backers want us to continue. They want to incorporate some of the film that was shot last night. So we may go in a little different direction."

She watched Mickey clean up his griddle.

"You do all of your cooking outside?"

"As long as it isn't raining or snowing."

89

"Amazing. Well, this show started as a competition. That's typical for reality shows. But I would like to ask you for more help to make this show *real*."

"What? What do you mean?" Mickey said.

She took a deep breath. "Here's the thing. The backers have too much invested to quit and want us to continue. But with Cliff's death, a silly competition sort of makes a mockery of that."

"So what are you thinking?" Frannie asked.

"I'm not really sure yet. First, I would like you to come over and meet our group because they would like to thank you, too. One possibility would be have you teach a few skills to them, like maybe how you cook those meals." She looked at Mickey. "The final program could contrast our first 24 hours with how the characters function after some instruction. Of course, there would be some pay involved, but then I would definitely have to ask you to sign a contract." She smiled. "How long are you staying here?"

"Today and tomorrow," Mickey said. "We leave Saturday morning."

"Well, would you come over and meet the group?"

"Sheriff Elliot wanted to talk to us…" Frannie said.

Larry nodded. "He does, but we'll be able to see him when he comes into the campground. We can go over for a few minutes."

"We need to clean things up here first," Jane Ann said.

Brandee frowned a little. "Just come over when you can, okay?"

Since most of the dishes and fixings came from Ferraros, Frannie helped Jane Ann carry them back into the Ferraro motor home.

"This is really bizarre," Frannie said. "Don't you think? I mean changing horses in midstream on a project like this?"

Jane Ann nodded. "I can't speak from experience, but I would think so." She put a stack of plates in the sink and ran a little dish water in. "You and I are probably not qualified to judge since this kind of sudden change of direction doesn't happen in a hospital or school. Who knows what goes on in Hollywood?"

Frannie grabbed a towel off a hook and dried the plates as Jane Ann washed. "And she's not very broken up about Cliff's death—or doesn't seem to be."

Jane Ann shrugged. "Maybe this is the opportunity she's been waiting for—to be the producer or director or whatever."

"Could be."

They joined the rest outside and walked together over to the rental encampment. A large group sat outside around a couple of picnic tables and in lawn chairs.

Tommy Pratt had his left arm in a cast but waved vigorously with his right. The man Madelyn and Chet had helped into their golf cart had crutches and a cast. A couple of people sported bandages, but there didn't appear to be any other serious injuries. Frannie did notice that they were better made up than most people in a campground.

Brandee held up her hand; rather unnecessary since everyone was already looking at them.

"I'd like to introduce you all to the people who helped us out in the storm last night." She nodded at Larry. "Would you mind telling us about your group and where you're from?"

Larry did and explained that they were on a tour of the UP and would be moving on Saturday. Brandee went on to introduce the participants. It seemed so scripted that Frannie glanced around, wondering if there was a camera on them somewhere. Sure enough, a young woman stood in the background, following the introductions with a camera on her shoulder.

They knew Tommy Pratt, of course, but were surprised to learn that since his childhood film career ended, he had completed an education degree and taught junior high science as well as coaching several sports at that level. And, as he'd told them, did occasional commercials.

"I've kept my hand in the movie business, though. I've produced a few science and coaching films."

The next woman, in her sixties, looked familiar, but Frannie didn't recognize her name, Shirley Joseph. She did recognize the black, furry ball in Shirley's lap — the dog that Larry had rescued from the collapsed tent.

"You may know me by my character name, Doris Dixon," Shirley said, giving them a sly smile.

"Ohmigosh!" Donna said. "My mom had all of your cookbooks."

"They weren't really my cookbooks, you know. They used my picture and I did the commercials." Doris Dixon was a character created by Acme Foods to sell cake mixes, flour, and numerous other food products.

Jane Ann laughed. "Doris Dixon may not have been a real person, but she was like a member of our family when we were kids."

"That's for sure," Mickey said. "I learned how to cook with your cake mixes."

Seated next to Shirley was a fit looking black woman. "Jaqui Dunbar. I ran sprint races in the '84 and 88 Olympics. I teach dance classes now and am a part time youth minister."

Tassi Ketchum and Cooper Wainwright sat next to Jaqui. Tassi waved her hand in a little wave. "We've sort of met. I'm on a morning TV show, *Koffee Klatch*."

"Oh, I've seen that!" Donna gushed. Frannie and Jane Ann just nodded because they had no idea what she was talking about.

Cooper Wainwright kept his introduction brief. "Coop Wainwright." Obviously, that was supposed to be sufficient.

An older man stood behind Wainwright's chair, arms crossed. "Gerard Fellows," he said. "Radio host — my show was *From Where I Sit*."

Frannie nodded. She remembered her mother listening to Gerard. The introductions continued and included three other actors—one fairly well known, the other two obscure—, a woman who had hosted a local children's TV show in Ohio, a Nebraska mayor who had made unsuccessful runs for the Senate and even one year for the Presidency, a retired hockey player—the man who had broken his leg the night before, and a Sixties pop singer who had been a one-hit wonder.

Larry saw the sheriff pull in at their campsites. "We need to go. After he's done with us, we're going up to see the Upper Falls, so we can talk to you when we get back," he said to Brandee.

She looked a little surprised, but nodded.

Walking back, Frannie said to him, "She can't believe we aren't jumping right on a chance for our fifteen minutes of fame."

"We're going to go back, aren't we?" Donna asked. "She asked for our help." Someone wanted their fifteen minutes.

"Later, probably," Larry said.

The sheriff had seen them coming and waited, hands on hips. Larry explained their visit.

"Well, I thank you, too, for your help last night." He took off his hat, rubbed his hand across his short hair, and restored the hat to its perch. "But we kind of got sidetracked on Mr. Remboski's death. I do need to ask you a few questions about that."

"We understand," Larry said.

"To refresh my memory, you met Mr. Rembowski briefly the night before last and had seen him arguing with two different men?"

"Yes," Frannie said. She thought about the people they just met. "We're pretty sure one was Cooper Wainwright. The man had the same build and it looked like the same shirt and hat as when we saw him later in the campground."

"That was Tuesday afternoon?"

Larry nodded. "But my wife and Mickey were the only ones who saw the argument yesterday morning."

Frannie said. "I was just thinking about that. We both thought the other man was shorter. When we just met the group, it was hard to tell height since most were sitting down. But maybe the radio guy — Fellows? He didn't look very tall and he does have lighter hair. Or the ex-mayor — Burnside?" She looked at Mickey.

"Could be, I guess."

The sheriff chuckled. "Let's hope we don't need an ID in court. Then, when you were on the cruise, can you tell me what happened?"

Rob said, "There's not much to tell. As the boat passed over the wreck, we saw his face, everybody kind of yelled, and the pilot stopped the boat. He called for help and moved the boat out of the way."

"Then we headed back as soon as the rescue people got there," Donna added. "That was it."

Frannie said, "You mentioned court. So he was murdered?"

"Not saying," the sheriff replied. He put his notebook back in his pocket. "If you think of anything else…"

"Sheriff, it just seems so strange that we saw him early that morning and he ends up in the Lake miles away. Did he drive over there? I assume he had a car here — did you find that?" Frannie asked.

The sheriff paused a moment. "We're still looking for his car. So, as I said, if there's anything else you think of to *tell* me, give me a call."

"Right," Larry said.

"Have a nice day."

CHAPTER ELEVEN

THURSDAY MORNING AND NOON

"I GUESS THAT MEANS we're dismissed," Mickey said, as they watched him drive away.

"Well, let's get out of here before something else happens." Larry jingled his truck keys.

"Can we all go in one vehicle?" Rob asked. "Or should I drive too?"

"We can squeeze in one," Jane Ann said. "It's not that far, right?"

"Right."

They grabbed water bottles and fanny packs and locked up their campers. The ride was only a couple of miles. Mickey did plenty of complaining with Jane Ann in his lap, but no one took him seriously. From the parking lot, a path led uphill to the collection of shops and restaurants arranged around a small open air deck.

"Shops first?" Donna said with a grin, once they had extracted themselves from the truck.

"No!" the men said in unison.

Donna laughed it off. "I figured."

They made a stop at the restrooms before starting up the wide, asphalt path leading to the falls. The climb was a little taxing, but they stopped frequently to rest and take pictures. Again, pines edged up to the path on both sides. The path turned when it reached the river and continued uphill. As they got closer, there were frequent viewing areas with wooden decks built out to view the falls.

"I can't believe this beautiful day after the ice storm last night," Jane Ann said.

A young couple with twin boys about four or five years old were just ahead of them. The boys climbed on the rail, jumped up and down, and spun in circles.

"What a waste," Mickey said.

"What?" Jane Ann asked.

"All of that energy. Those kids don't need all of that—we could use some of it." They all agreed.

At the third viewing platform, one of the boys said, "Mom! How many waterfalls are there?"

"Just one. It's the same one we saw at the last place."

"No! This one's bigger!"

Mickey raised his eyebrows at the rest. "He's right, you know. It's bigger," he said in a low voice.

The other twin disagreed, however, and they raced on ahead, arguing all the way.

At the end of the path, they took a break on the benches provided and brought out their water bottles. This point looked down over the falls and a long wooden staircase led down for a closer view. Signs warned of slippery steps because of the mist generated by the falls.

After a rest, Rob said, "I'm ready for the steps. Who's with me?"

Mickey, who had breathing problems from many years of smoking, declined.

Frannie said, "My knee's a little sore from that hill. I'll stay here and babysit Mick."

Larry, Donna, and Jane Ann said they would join Rob, so Frannie gave her camera to Larry. Mickey and Frannie sat enjoying the warmth of the sun and laughing about nothing. They hadn't been there very long when they spotted a group coming up the trail. As they got closer, Mickey whispered "It's the 'celebrities.'"

"You're right."

Shirley Joseph was at the front with Brandee Tudor. Frannie spotted Gerard Fellows and Taylor Burnside in the group. Jaqui Dunbar was bouncing along looking not the least bit tired, but Cooper Wainwright looked in worse shape than Mickey.

When the group arrived, Brandee expressed surprise at running in to them, although they had told her they were coming up here. Frannie explained the absence of the rest of her group and pointed at the stairs.

Cooper, Shirley, and two of the actors whose names Frannie couldn't remember elected to stay at the waiting area while the rest started down the steps.

Shirley sat down by Frannie. "This really is a beautiful place. Is this your first time here?"

"Yes it is, and we are loving it."

"But you camp lot, I guess?"

"We do. Lots of short trips in the summer with these friends and others. Longer trips in the fall and spring by ourselves or with Mickey and Jane Ann."

"It sounds great. My husband doesn't like to travel and I'm sure I could never get him to camp, even in a motor home, but I do take trips with friends." She leaned back against the wooden bench back. "The sun feels wonderful."

Cooper looked at his watch. "How long does it take to get down those steps and back?"

"I don't know. Our group's probably been gone about twenty minutes," Frannie answered.

Just then they heard arguing voices and the twin boys popped up the stairs.

"You could *not* swim over those falls!"

"I could too. Maybe not those ones, but I could swim over the first ones we saw. The *small* ones."

"They're the same!"

"No, they're not!"

The parents appeared behind them, shaking their heads. "Boys, please, quit your arguing," said the mother.

"But he's wrong. He said…" And off they went down the hill.

Shirley laughed. "Oh, my. I certainly don't have the energy for *that* any more."

Frannie was just going to ask her if she had children when they heard screams.

Mickey and Frannie rushed to the top of the stairs and peered over the railing. Larry, Donna, Jane Ann, and Rob were on their way back up, but at the next landing, they could see Jaqui Dunbar hanging from the railing. Brandee and Gerard Fellows were bent over the railing, grabbing her arms. Rob and Jane Ann got there first and helped to haul her back up. Larry and Taylor Burnside helped her up the steps.

They got her seated on one of the benches, and Shirley offered her a bandana to wipe her face. Jaqui was shaking and crying. Both groups crowded around her until Larry got them to back away, leaving Shirley and Brandee on either side of her.

"What happened?" Frannie asked.

"We didn't see anything," Larry said. "They were going down and we had just passed them on our way back up."

Jaqui looked up at them. "I was pushed! Gerard was behind me." She glared at the radio host.

He held up his hands. "It wasn't me! Someone tripped me and I fell into you!"

Brandee Tudor wiped her forehead and straightened her ball cap. "I'm sure it was an accident, how ever it happened. Jaqui, do you have some water? You can rest here, or we could go back and wait for the others at the cafe."

"I think I'll go back." She shuddered.

Jane Ann spoke up. "We're walking that way now. We'll be glad to accompany her, and you can wait for the rest of your group, Brandee."

"Oh. Yeah. Okay, that'd be great. We shouldn't be long—I think we're just waiting for two." She counted heads. "Yeah, Tommy and Misty. I guess anyone else who wants to go back can." She looked around the group, and slowly the others got up to follow.

Frannie and Jane Ann walked with Jaqui between them in case she felt faint. Fortunately, it was all downhill. With the group behind them, Frannie felt a little like she had with a class of eighth graders on a field trip back when she was teaching.

Jaqui glanced over her shoulder every once in a while as if she was afraid of something.

"Are you okay?" Frannie asked her.

"Yeah, yeah. Just makes me kind of nervous. I know I was pushed."

Frannie caught Jane Ann's eye over Jaqui's head. "I hope not," Frannie said.

Conversation picked up in the group behind them. Gerard Fellows was entertaining the others with stories of his radio days. By the time they reached the parking lot and shops, everyone had relaxed except Jaqui. Her bearing said she wasn't going to let her guard down soon.

Jane Ann claimed a big round umbrella table on the open air deck.

"Jaqui, can I get you something to drink? Water, soda, iced tea?" Frannie asked.

Jaqui broke a little smile. "Maybe if they have a lemonade? If not, water or iced tea would be fine."

Donna said, "I'm going to check out that boutique over there. I see some cute shirts."

As Frannie left, she heard Mickey start to quiz Jaqui about her Olympic experiences. Larry followed his wife with more drink orders.

"That was strange," she said to Larry as they stood in line. "Do you think she really was pushed?"

He shrugged. "It was pretty crowded on those stairs. Seems more likely that it was just an accident."

"This is really getting weird. I don't think I want to hang out with 'celebrities' much."

They gave their order at a window. The clerk put the drinks on two trays for them, and they returned to the table. Jaqui brightened as she sipped the lemonade.

"This hits the spot. Thank you again." She looked around and grimaced. "This is a lovely place, but now I'm sorry I got into this."

"Several have said that," Frannie said. "Why?"

Jaqui looked surprised that Frannie would even ask. She counted off on her fingers. "First, Cliff's death. And I saw him leave that morning—who knew it would be the last time? He drove out right before Brandee went to get donuts. The ice storm last night, and then getting pushed today." She shook her head in disbelief.

Frannie was going to ask her more about seeing Cliff, but Brandee Tudor arrived with Tommy Pratt and Misty something—one of the actresses. By this time, the two groups filled up three tables.

Brandee took Donna's empty chair. "We haven't had any more chance to talk, but would you guys be able to demonstrate starting a fire and cooking on it this evening? I can get whatever groceries you need."

Mickey said, "For the whole group you mean?"

"Is that doable?"

103

Mickey looked at his watch. "Nothing fancy. We could do burgers."

Brandee raised her eyebrows. "Do you usually do fancy?"

"Sometimes. We've done Steak Florentine and paella and smoked brisket and—"

She held up her hands. "Okay, okay. I get it. Burgers would be fine. You need to make a list for me. We may have what we need in the freezer truck."

"Can you do veggie burgers?" Jaqui asked.

"I *know* there's some of those in the truck," Brandee said. "That's my preference too."

Donna came bustling back from the boutique with two large sacks.

Rob rolled his eyes. "You know our camper's only twenty-eight foot, right?" That got some laughs.

Mickey stood up. "Time to get going and get busy."

"Thank you so much," Brandee said.

CHAPTER TWELVE
THURSDAY AFTERNOON

ALL THE WAY BACK to the campground, Mickey organized them.

"We'll need at least two of our grills. Girls, you need to come up with a couple of simple sides, see what we need for them, and get a list to Brandee. I think the nearest grocery is about thirty miles away, so keep that in mind."

"Lord, you're bossy," Frannie said.

"It's called leadership."

The campground was quiet when they returned. The celebrities were being transported in a chartered bus.

"If Rob and I get our grills out, you can just leave yours here," Larry said. Each of the couples had the same handy grill system which assembled easily and suspended from a single post, driven into the ground.

"Good idea," Mickey said. He pulled a small notebook and pen out of his shirt pocket and sat down at the picnic table. "Okay. We'll tell her to take care of the burgers and buns. Condiments?"

Donna raised her hand. "I'll do that. I have cheese slices and onions, too. No pickles or tomatoes though."

"We've got tomatoes," Jane Ann said. "*Lots* of tomatoes. We cleaned out the garden before we left."

Frannie added, "And we have pickles."

"How about cowboy beans in the Dutch oven?" Rob asked.

"And coleslaw?" Donna said.

"S'mores for dessert," Mickey finished. "The perfect camping supper. Jane Ann, decide on a coleslaw recipe and Frannie, you make the grocery list."

"What are you going to be doing?" Frannie asked.

He pointed at his head. "Thinking. I am the brains of this outfit."

"Now we're in trouble," Larry said, as he went to one of his storage compartments for his grill.

FRANNIE FOLLOWED DONNA to their camper to check on her stock of condiments.

"Ketchup's a little low — maybe another bottle of that."

Frannie wrote it down and went to find Jane Ann. She had a small camping cookbook out. "How about a coleslaw with walnuts, craisins and apples?"

"Sounds great!" Frannie added the ingredients to her list and went back outside.

Rob got out his grill and his cast-iron Dutch oven. He told her what he needed for his cowboy beans. She also added marshmallows, graham crackers, and Hershey bars to the list for S'mores. She had another inspiration. She went in to check her pantry and found both miniature marshmallows and mini-chocolate chips. Perfect. She added bananas to the list. The campers would have a dessert choice of S'mores or banana boats. Or both.

She took the list over to Brandee, who looked it over. "Do you want to go with me?"

"Not really," Frannie said. "To be honest, I'm not fully recovered from yesterday and last night. I need a little rest this afternoon."

"Of course." Brandee looked as if she remembered suddenly how *old* these people were.

Frannie did want a nap but also felt if they were going to be responsible for supper, she didn't need to go on a two-hour grocery run.

"I assume you have your own vehicle here?" Frannie asked. Brandee nodded.

"Does anyone else?"

"Have a vehicle? Well, of course, Cliff did, and almost all of the production staff do. Why?"

"You know, Mickey and I heard Cliff arguing with someone early Wednesday morning, and then he ended up miles away. Is his car still here?"

Brandee reverted to her haughtier persona. "What do you mean? I didn't notice."

"I'm sure the sheriff checked. But none of your 'celebrities' have cars here do they?"

Brandee looked very puzzled. "No. What are you getting at?"

"Just wondering how Cliff got to the lake, that's all. If he was alive when he left here. If he drove himself. Doesn't make much sense."

Brandee stared at her with an open mouth.

"Never mind," Frannie said. "I'll get out of your way so you can make the grocery run. Do you want to cook supper here or in the tent area?"

"Um, I don't think anyone's going to willingly go back to the tent area—at least not tonight. I want the participants to do the cooking, so you just get them started, okay? We'll do it all outside."

"Okay, that should work fine. I'll see you later."

When Frannie glanced back, Brandee still stared at her, but quickly turned and headed to her trailer. She was certainly an odd duck and could change personality at will. Frannie didn't know what to think of her. On the way, Frannie tried to think who all was in the tent area when she helped Tassi with the fire. Since she hadn't met most of them at the time, it was hard to remember. But then she thought about what Jaqui had said earlier about seeing Cliff leave that fateful morning. So he had left of his own accord.

A NAP, FOLLOWED BY A SHOWER, was just the ticket. As Frannie left the shower house, she noticed people milling around in the rental RV area. When she got back to her own campsite, the men were collecting items needed for the supper preparation.

Mickey, of course, took charge. "We need to get fires going, so they're ready to cook on when Brandee gets back."

Rob put his Dutch oven on the table. "We forgot to ask if she has firewood, but I have two bins in my truck. Let's load everything else in there."

Donna put a bin with the condiments in the back of the truck and Jane Ann added a sack of tomatoes. Frannie found a couple of old vinyl table cloths to include plus her jar of pickles. Rob drove the truck over and the rest walked.

Tassi Ketchum sat at one of the picnic tables filing her nails and barely glanced up when they arrived. But when Rob and Larry hauled the bins of firewood out of the truck, she jumped up and stuck her emery board in her back pocket.

"Are you going to build a fire? Can I help?"

Frannie smiled to herself. Tassi probably considered herself an expert based on Frannie's slapdash instruction. Mickey and Larry would straighten her out in a hurry. And end up in a big argument with each other.

The guys, of course, were much nicer to Tassi than they ever were to each other. Gerard Fellows got into the act as well, and was especially interested in assembly of the grills.

Rob put a pipe with a stake attached into the ground next to the fire ring and used a second, longer pipe to pound it in. A short pipe placed through the top of the vertical one held a chain threaded through that which held the grill.

"Wow!" Gerard said. "That is slick." He watched Larry get out the other one. "Can I put that one together?"

"See?" Mickey laughed. "It's just like Tom Sawyer painting the fence."

Shirley Joseph joined the group. "Is there anything I can do?"

Mickey grinned at her. "Now's our chance to see if Doris Dixon can actually cook."

"I don't think there's much food prep we can do until Brandee gets back with the groceries," Jane Ann said. "But here's the recipe for the coleslaw when she does."

THEY MANAGED TO KEEP people busy setting the table and doing some prep. Misty sliced the tomatoes, almost nicking her fingers in the process. Several worked while favoring injuries from the night before. Brandee pulled into the area in her old yellow compact and recruited some of the celebrities to help unload the groceries.

For the next hour, Larry and Mickey gave instructions on fire-building—not the same instructions of course, since they had never agreed on that—and then the burger cooking. Rob supervised Tassi and Cooper on the cowboy beans. Jane Ann and Donna directed Shirley and Tommy on the coleslaw, and Frannie ran a small workshop to prepare the banana boats.

The camera people, Kasey, Wyatt, and Bryce, darted in and out, catching closeups and panning back to take in the whole busy site. There were apparently enough 'whoopses' and disagreements to keep Brandee happy, since she didn't add any artificial stresses. At one point, a buzzing noise caused Frannie to look up. A drone hovered above the clearing.

Wyatt, a scrawny kid with a camera on his shoulder, leaned over her. "Ma'am, please don't look up at the camera."

"Camera?" She, of course, looked up again and then said, "Oops. Sorry."

When Frannie's group finished their foil-wrapped banana boats and stacked them on a tray, Frannie said to Brandee, "Did you notice whether Cliff's car is still in the lot?"

She sighed, obviously tired of hearing about the car. "No, I don't think it's there."

Frannie nodded and went to check on the griller team. Gerard leaned forward in a lawn chair, watching the fire and the burgers. Frannie took an empty chair beside him.

"This is really great," Gerard said to her. "Too bad you guys weren't advising Cliff during the planning stages." He frowned. "He probably wouldn't have listened, though."

"Did you work with him often?"

He sighed. "I tried. He said he would back a project of mine and produce it, but backed out at the last minute. Nearly cost me my house."

111

"Oh, that's awful!"

"Yeah, he was pretty self-centered and didn't care who he hurt." He bent over and picked up a stick to poke the fire, but the anger was clear on his face.

"I'm sorry to hear that, Gerard. How did you become involved with this project then?"

He gave a sly smile. "Shirley. We've been friends for years and she told Cliff that she wouldn't do it unless I did. He probably thought he could give me some extra grief—and he did. The tent he gave me the other night was missing two of the main poles. I rigged it up by a tree."

"I saw that! That was very clever. Good luck with your cooking—the burgers look great!" Frannie got up and walked around the fire where Larry and Mickey were conferring.

"I'm going over to the restroom," she said to Larry. "Anything you guys need from our camper?"

"No, we're good. Should be able to eat in fifteen or twenty minutes." He rolled his eyes at her as Gerard flipped a burger into the fire. "That's the third one," he muttered.

Frannie grinned and then headed across the campground. She thought about the drone and the other cameras. Maybe the sheriff wasn't aware of those, and that film could be helpful. She'd have Larry call him.

SUPPER WENT WELL. It was pretty simple on the Shoemaker-Ferraro scale of meals, but the celebrities raved. Frannie figured they were getting pretty hungry after a couple of nights of their own efforts. Afterwards, Brandee assigned Misty, Gerard, and the woman host from children's TV to do the dishes.

Larry and Rob supervised building up one of the fires while others pulled their chairs around. Mickey retrieved his guitar from Rob's truck and began a group sing. Cooper Wainwright hung back, leaning against one of the motor homes with his arms folded, watching the efforts with a look of disdain.

Finally, Tassi yelled, "Coop! Where's *your* guitar?"

The rest broke into a chant, including Mickey. "We want Coop! We want Coop!"

He tried to look unimpressed, but a little smile broke through. Tassi came over and gave him a pleading look and that did it. He raised his hands. "Okay, Okay." He went to one of the motor homes and came back out with a guitar case.

He took a chair next to Mickey, who was putting his own guitar away.

"No, man," Cooper said to him. "Or are you too proud to play with anyone else?"

Mickey grinned. "I didn't figure we had the same repertoire."

"You don't know much about my music then." He started off with "She'll Be Comin' Round the Mountain" and Mickey joined right in. They rolled through some Woody Guthrie, Dylan, and Mellencamp. Cooper moved on to Johnny Cash and other old country songs. The

113

group joined in on the familiar songs. Frannie thought it was a perfect evening to give newbies a taste of camping. She no longer noticed the swooping cameramen or the drone.

Amber Gold spent most of the evening on her phone, her blonde straight hair curtaining her face. At one point between songs, she looked up and shouted, "Guys! Listen to this. A local news station said the sheriff's department is treating Cliff's death as a homicide." She dropped her jaw in a dramatic gesture and scanned the circle.

LATER, FRANNIE AND JANE ANN came back from a trip to the shower house and were about to rejoin the group when Frannie heard low voices coming from behind one of the motor homes. She grabbed Jane Ann's arm and stopped her. She put her finger to her lips and jerked her head in the direction of the voices. They stood quietly facing the group around the fire like they were listening to the music at a distance.

"I deserve this chance," they heard Brandee say.

"Chance is the right word." A man's voice Frannie didn't recognize. "These investors aren't interested in a chancy thing. They put money up because Cliff has—had —a solid reputation. Baird McKewn will be here by tomorrow afternoon to take over and that's final. You'll have to get your experience on someone else's dime."

They heard a car door slam and a powerful engine start up. Headlights appeared illuminating the way for a sporty car to the campground exit.

Muffled sobs came from the other side of the RV, and Jane Ann pulled Frannie back toward the campfire.

They returned to their chairs, and Jane Ann leaned over. "I think Brandee just got fired."

Frannie nodded. "Here she comes," she whispered.

Brandee came around the end of the motor home. She wiped her eyes, but her face conveyed fury rather than sadness. She stalked over to the rental she was using, went inside and slammed the door.

Frannie noticed one of the cameras followed her.

LATER, ON THE WAY BACK to their camper, Frannie said, "Larry, I wonder if Sheriff Elliot has checked all the films for any hint of what happened to Cliff?"

"I would think so. He's interviewed the participants."

"Do you suppose he knows about the drone?"

"I'll mention it, next time we see him."

He obviously didn't think it was urgent.

CHAPTER THIRTEEN

FRIDAY MORNING

ANOTHER STRESSFUL DAY resulted in a sound night's sleep. Frannie woke the next morning feeling quite refreshed until she remembered Cliff's death and Jaqui's accident. This would be their last day at Ojibway Falls and she hoped not too much of it was taken up with the antics of the reality show. And, of course, that the calamities were over.

It was cloudy but dry, and the group had their breakfast out of the way before they saw any sign of activity from the celebrities.

"For our last night here, I suggest we try out the restaurant at the Upper Falls, the Motley Moose. It's supposed to be pretty good," Mickey said.

"Oh, wow!" Frannie said. "Eat out? Sounds good to me."

Mickey looked offended. "You don't like my cooking?"

"Of course I like yours. I'm just tired of my own."

An old, rusty blue pickup pulled in at their site, and a young woman with flaming red curls got out.

"Isn't that—?" Larry looked at Frannie.

She nodded. "The girl you pulled out of the river. She was on the glass-bottom boat tour, too."

The woman approached. "Hi." She twisted a curl around her finger. "I think you are the people who helped me the other day? Saved my life, really." She looked at them expectantly.

Rob stood up and walked over to shake her hand. "Rob Nowak. We were just glad we happened to be there at the right time."

"Um, well, thank you so much! I would have stopped sooner, but I just found out you were in this campground. I'm Vernelle Vosburg." Her pale, freckled skin verified that her hair was a natural color. Her upturned nose gave her a perky look.

"Do you live near here?" Larry asked.

She shook her head. "I'm from southern Ohio. But I love to canoe and kayak and I've wanted to come up here for a long time. I'm camped over in the other campground away from the river. There weren't any sites left here. Hey! Weren't you guys on that cruise when they found that guy?"

"Yes, we were," Frannie said. "I thought that was you."

Vernelle pushed her hair out of her face. "Man. That was something, wasn't it? You didn't know him, did you?"

Frannie explained about Cliff and the reality show.

"Wow! Can I sit down? That's a lot to take in."

"Sure." Frannie pulled a lawn chair around for her.

117

"I think I saw him earlier that morning. 'Course, it's hard to tell." She grimaced. "He didn't exactly look…" She shrugged, hands palms up.

Frannie frowned. "You saw him earlier? Where?"

"Frannie," Larry warned.

Vernelle ignored him. "I was hiking along the cliff. I'd parked my truck at a public parking lot, you know, across from that island where the wreck was? I took a path that led to a small waterfall. It was on the hike that I saw one of the glass-bottom boats go by and thought that would be fun to do."

"But you saw Cliff—?"

Vernelle cocked her head. "What do you mean? I was hiking *along* the cliff."

Frannie smiled. "That was the guy's name—Cliff Remboski."

"Oh, really? Yeah. Well, he was arguing with someone."

"What time was that, do you remember?"

"Hmmm. Must have been around 9:00 or 9:30, maybe. I think it was about 8:30 when I left the campground. I hadn't been on the path for very long."

"Did you see who he was arguing with?" Jane Ann asked.

"Not very well. There were a lot of trees. He was facing me and I saw that silver hair."

Frannie persisted and ignored Larry's disapproval. "So, the other person—a man or a woman?"

Vernelle squinted her eyes and cocked her head. "I really don't know. Why does this matter? What are all of these questions for?"

Frannie straightened up. "He might have been murdered."

"Murdered?" Vernelle paled and put her hand to her chest. "Oh my gosh. You aren't accusing me, are you?"

"No, no. Of course not." Frannie patted her hand.

Larry stood and walked around behind Frannie. For emphasis, she thought. "The sheriff has *never* said that it was anything but an accident."

"Right," Frannie agreed, "but he's awfully interested in any arguments Cliff had. Why would he care if it was an accident? And Amber said it was on the news that they are treating it like a homicide." She turned back to Vernelle. "Have you told the sheriff what you saw?"

"No, I haven't talked to him. Do you think I should call him?"

Larry nodded. "Yes, you definitely need to. Otherwise you're withholding information."

"I guess I never thought of it, because I thought it was an accident. I'll do that." Vernelle stood up. "I should get going. I've got a spot reserved in a kayak tour of the Pictured Rock area. I was just fascinated by that place the other day and want to take a more leisurely tour. I certainly won't be doing it in my own canoe." She grimaced and pulled out her phone. "Here's what it looked like after they pulled it out. I can't believe that I did something so stupid. My insurance company will

119

probably have a fit." She showed the photo around to the group.

"Wow!" Mickey said. "Just remember that you would have looked like that if you had still been in it."

"You're right. And I have you people to thank for that. Well, have a good day." She headed back to her truck and drove off.

"Curiouser and curiouser," Frannie said.

Jane Ann agreed. "I wonder if it was the same mystery person you saw arguing with him?"

"You mean, maybe he followed Cliff and continued the fight?"

"Seems logical. We know Cliff had an argument with Cooper Wainwright the day before, and then the person you and Mickey saw. How many different people was he likely to be fighting with in less than twenty-four hours?"

"Good point," Frannie said.

Larry shook his head. "Don't you ladies have some thing else to do besides speculate about murder? Like maybe wait on your husbands?"

Frannie looked at Jane Ann. "Speaking of murder...."

"As a distraction, what do we want to do today?" Mickey asked.

"Laundry?" Jane Ann said.

"Shopping?" Donna suggested.

Mickey threw up his hands. "I might as well have asked Cuba." Cuba perked up from her spot behind Frannie's chair and came over to lay her head on Mickey's knee.

Rob leaned back in his chair. "Are we committed to helping the 'celebrities ' any more?"

Mickey grinned. "We never did get a contract so I don't think we're obligated in any way."

"I don't believe any contract will be forthcoming from Brandee." She repeated the conversation she and Jane Ann had overheard the night before.

"Hoo boy," Mickey said, shaking his head. "I bet she's not happy. Have you seen her this morning?"

"No sign of her," Jane Ann said. "The new director or producer or whatever isn't supposed to be here until the afternoon. I was serious about laundry. I think there's a laundry in the little shop area at the Upper Falls."

"I could do some, too," Frannie said.

Larry frowned. "I was thinking about doing some fishing."

"We hardly need you guys to do a couple loads of laundry."

"Cool."

Frannie rolled her eyes. "Poor browbeaten husband. How about you, Donna?"

"You mean, do I want a browbeaten husband? I already have one. Just ask him."

"Laundry, silly."

"I can probably scare up a load. And then check out some of the other shops while it runs." She grinned.

"I lost my billfold," Rob said. "I don't have any more money."

"Relax. I carry my own."

121

Frannie brought out their collapsible hamper, full to the brim, along with a jug of detergent and a bag of quarters, and put the hamper in the back of their truck. Jane Ann had already loaded her laundry, and Donna came dragging a huge garbage bag.

Frannie laughed. "That's what you call 'scaring up a load'? You must have been really frightening."

Donna shrugged. "You know how it is. You grab a few clothes, notice the towels, then think you might as well do the sheets, then you see jackets still damp from the other night, and so on."

Jane Ann helped her get the bag into the truck and the three of them piled in. Frannie spent about five minutes adjusting the seat and the mirrors due to about ten inches difference between Larry's height and hers. Finally, she got her seatbelt on and started the truck. She pulled forward with a jerk.

She grimaced. "Gas pedal sticks. Not as smooth as my car."

"Just don't forget this truck is a lot bigger than your car, too." Jane Ann laughed.

Despite the unwieldy feeling of the vehicle compared to what she was used to driving, Frannie managed to navigate to the campground entrance and out to the road. The entrance was located on a curve and because of that and the pines growing almost up to the highway, visibility to her right was poor.

"I think you're clear," Jane Ann said. Frannie edged out to the left when Jane Ann said, "Here comes someone. Gun it!"

They sped forward with a lurch. Donna looked back through the rear window to check on the approaching vehicle.

"Oh-oh."

Frannie panicked and looked up at the rear view mirror. "What?"

"Your hamper and Jane Ann's are spilled all over the pickup bed. Should have used a garbage bag."

"Is that all?" Frannie gasped in relief.

"It's really a mess," Donna insisted.

"Yeah, but better than being flattened by a semi or a road grader or something."

"You're right. Sorry."

"I don't think the guys have nearly as much as excitement on their trips as we do," Jane Ann said, as they turned in to the Upper Falls access road. Frannie parked near the laundry at the lower level of the shops.

Donna said, "I can't get out. The door's locked."

Frannie hit the master lock. "Sorry. It's those damn child locks. We had them turned off but then turned them back on when the kids visited this summer." She got out of the truck and peered over the side of the bed.

"Oh, man."

Jane Ann joined her and they both surveyed the chaos. Socks sprouted from the woodbox and underwear was twisted in the extra lawn chairs. Frannie's favorite blue shirt peeked out from behind a cooler.

"I guess maybe we're lucky it didn't all blow out of the truck completely," Jane Ann said with a grimace.

"Maybe some of it did. How will we ever know?"

Donna lowered the tail gate and pulled out her garbage bag, still intact. "Do you want help picking it up?"

Frannie shook her head. "You go on and get started. Our bad—we'll take care of it."

Donna dragged her heavy bag into the laundry. Jane Ann watched her go before climbing up into the bed. "Write this date down."

"Why?"

"The day Donna used more common sense than *either* you or me."

"So true." Frannie got her knee up on the tailgate, and Jane Ann gave her a hand to pull her up. They worked quickly, refilling their hampers, and handing off items that belonged to the other couple. Jane Ann slid down off the tailgate, and Frannie handed her the hampers.

By the time they got into the laundry, Donna had her washers going. She hefted her purse from the floor. "I'm going up to the shops."

"We'll catch up," Jane Ann said. "There aren't that many—we'll find you."

They filled two machines apiece and placed their hampers in front of the machines.

"Shall we go find Donna?" Jane Ann said.

"Absolutely. I think she could teach us a thing or two about shopping. I'm sort of retail challenged."

They headed up the steps to the open patio ringed by shops and a couple of restaurants—one the Motley Moose that Mickey had suggested. The first shop held a single narrow aisle of tee shirts and touristy souvenirs.

"I don't see her in there," Frannie said.

The next shop sold sporting goods and Frannie and Jane Ann knew she wouldn't be there. But they were successful with the third—a boutique of home accessories. Donna stood at the check out counter and waved them in.

"Look at these cute magnets about camping! I got one for each of you, too! And check out those placemats. Love the colors!"

Frannie and Jane Ann each took a magnet that said *Take a Hike!* "Thanks, Donna. This is a great message for Larry when he gets too bossy. I can just point to it."

"Do you want to look around here or go on to the bookstore?"

"Can't resist a bookstore," Jane Ann said. "I don't have room for any more decorative items in my camper or my house!"

They browsed the small bookstore. Frannie picked up the latest Louise Penny mystery and Jane Ann got a small guidebook to the UP. "This doesn't add to my clutter. I can keep it in my purse," she explained.

Frannie looked at her watch. "The wash should be done. We'd better go put it in the dryers."

They traipsed back down the steps and moved their laundry.

125

"Anyplace else you wanted to look, Donna?" Jane Ann asked. "Otherwise I suggest a beverage at the Motley Moose and we can make a reservations for tonight at the same time."

"Fine with me," Donna said.

CHAPTER FOURTEEN
FRIDAY NOON

THE DARK INTERIOR of the restaurant was a welcome relief from the bright sun. They selected a table near the windows and while they waited for the waitress, looked around at the rustic decor. Log walls and a peaked plank ceiling were accented by heavy, hammered beams. An odd mix of what appeared to be real trophy heads of bears, deer and buffalo with obvious toy stuffed-animal versions hung on the walls. A young woman with light brown hair tucked under a perky cap approached then with a pencil and order pad.

She followed their stares at the walls. "None of them are real."

"Not even the ones that look real?" Donna asked.

"Nope." She smiled. "What would you like today? Want to see a menu?"

"I don't think we need one," Frannie said. "I'd just like coffee."

Jane Ann ordered iced tea.

Donna cocked her head and squinted at the advertisements above the bar. "Do you have lemonade?"

"Yes, we do. Large or small?"

"Oh, large. Shopping makes me thirsty."

The waitress stuck the pencil behind her ear. "I'll be right back with your order."

Frannie had been scanning a blackboard listing the daily specials. "They have a couple kinds of fish and that pasta looks good."

"And they have pasties, too," Donna said.

"So when we get back, what's our plan for the afternoon?"

Jane Ann said, "There's a trail that runs down river, away from the falls. Might be interesting."

"We could just kick back and cool it," Donna said, "Play some dominos."

Frannie got up. "That sounds okay by me. Maybe if we stay at our campsite, nothing bad will happen. I'm going to hit the restroom before I start my coffee. Be right back."

She found the women's off to the side of the bar. When she came back out, she noticed the only person sitting at the bar. Brandee Tudor leaned on her elbows. She had a squat glass with what looked like straight whiskey sitting in front of her and a glazed expression on her face. A little early for that.

"Hi Brandee. How are you doing this morning?"

Brandee looked up and Frannie realized her eyes were swollen and red. "What's the matter?"

"Wha—?" Brandee showed no recognition

"Frannie Shoemaker. From the campground."

"Oh. 'Spose you want your money."

Frannie shook her head. "No, just wondering if you're okay. It's kind of early to be drinking." She nodded at the glass.

"None a yer bizness," Brandee slurred. "Yer that nosy one, right?"

"Sorry I bothered you." Frannie returned to her table.

"Is that Brandee?" Donna asked.

"Yes, and pretty drunk, I would say. She thought I was there to collect money from her."

"For what? Oh, that non-existent contract?" Jane Ann said.

"I guess." Frannie sipped her coffee. "Good thing we weren't depending on it for our groceries. I'm guessing that she was counting on taking over Cliff's job, and we know that didn't happen."

Donna shook her head. "I feel sorry for her."

"I wonder if she's driving," Jane Ann said.

"We'd better make sure she doesn't." Frannie thought a moment. "Why don't I go down and get my clothes out of the dryer while you guys keep an eye on her? Then I'll come back and watch while you do the same. If she starts to leave, we'll try and talk her into riding with us — or one of you could drive her."

They agreed with the plan. Frannie handed Jane Ann money for her coffee and headed back to the laundry. When she returned, Jane Ann and Donna went to take care of their clothes. Brandee continued to sit at the bar, although Frannie didn't see her order any refills. Actually the bartender, a college-aged young man, seemed to be keeping a pretty close eye on her.

Brandee turned, spotted Frannie, slipped off the stool, and went down the hall to the restroom. Her movements were deliberate and slow. Frannie waited for her to come back and thought she would try to talk to her again.

Jane Ann and Donna were back before Brandee reappeared.

"We put our hampers in the back seat of the truck so they won't fall over on the way back. What happened to Brandee?" Jane Ann asked, after spotting the empty stool.

"She went to the restroom. Maybe she's getting rid of some of that. Although," Frannie glanced at her watch, "it's been a while. Oh, no—"

"What?" Donna slurped the last of her lemonade.

"I think there's an outside door back there." Frannie jumped up and hurried toward the hallway. The little hall turned out of sight, but when Frannie rounded the corner, her suspicions were confirmed. The exit door stood open. She leaned out of the door in time to see Brandee's battered yellow compact pull away from the parking lot, not exactly in a straight line.

She hurried back to the table. "Ladies! C'mon, she went out a back door!" They left money for the waitress and made a beeline for the parking lot.

Frannie's exit from the parking lot at the wheel of the truck wasn't much smoother than Brandee's. But they were too late. They rounded a curve in the access road to see the nose of Brandee's car pancaked against a tree.

"Oh, no!" Donna said from the back seat. Just then the driver's door opened and Brandee's head appeared slowly. Frannie slowed and pulled to the side. Jane Ann was the first one to the car. She pulled the driver's door open farther and got Brandee under the arms to help her out.

The ubiquitous ball cap was gone and Brandee's dishwater blond hair spilled on her shoulders. Her bewildered eyes took in the smashed front of the car and the women gathered around her.

"Are you okay?" Jane Ann said. "Do you hurt anywhere?"

Brandee hiccuped and shook her head.

"We'll give you a ride back to the campground and you can call a tow truck. This car isn't going anywhere on its own."

Tears ran down the woman's cheeks. "Everything is awful. First Cliff and then my job. I can't afford to fix this." She waved her hand at the car.

"Don't you have insurance?" Donna asked.

Brandee shook her head. "Couldn't 'ford it."

Frannie caught Jane Ann's eye over Brandee's head. She was still drunk and that would just add to her woes. Frannie knew what Larry would say, but still, there was no point in standing around on this narrow road.

"Donna, is there room to shove those hampers over so there's a space for Brandee?"

"We can make it work." Donna trudged up the side of the ditch to the road and the truck. She tugged and

131

pushed one of the hampers and Frannie helped her wedge it between the seats on the floor so they could move other one over. Jane Ann guided Brandee to the truck and helped her into the back seat.

"My purse!" Brandy whined, after she got seated.

"I'll get it." Frannie sidestepped back down the ditch to the driver's door. She spotted the purse on the floor in front of the passenger seat, half spilled. Scooping the contents back into the purse was something of a gymnastics feat almost beyond her ability. She grabbed the keys out of the ignition before she exited the car.

Back at the truck, she hoisted herself into the driver's seat of the truck and handed the purse back to Brandee. Larry would never object to her helping an accident victim—even if it was self-created—but he would insist on Brandee following the law. So as she pulled out, she said over her shoulder, "You'll have to call the sheriff, too, and report it."

"Why? No one else was involved. No one was hurt."

"You could get charged with leaving the scene of an accident." Frannie wasn't sure, but thought she heard Brandee say in a low voice, "Not if they don't catch me." She glanced at Jane Ann for confirmation. Jane Ann raised her eyebrows and shrugged.

"My husband is a retired cop," Frannie went on. "He can tell you what you need to do."

There was no response from Brandee. Donna filled the silence, chattering about how exciting *Celebrity Campout* was going to be.

On their return, Frannie said to Brandee, "I'll see if Larry's inside. Do you need a phone?" Brandee shook her head. Frannie, Jane Ann, and Donna lugged their laundry to their campers.

Larry was fixing himself a cup of coffee.

"Did you already get all of the fish cleaned?" She grinned at him.

He brushed her query off. "It was a nice morning."

"Probably better than the little women having to beat the laundry on the rocks in the ice cold water, crippling our hands." She made a claw with one hand and waved it in front of his face. "On a more serious note, Brandee Tudor literally had a run-in with a tree this morning." She described the events leading up to Brandee's crash.

He frowned. "Did you call the sheriff?"

"No, I told her she had to, and she said she would. She said she didn't need to borrow a phone. I assume she's doing that now."

He peered out the window. "Where is she? Did she leave?"

Frannie opened the door to get a better view. "Maybe she went back to her RV?"

Larry took her by the shoulders. "Look, you are the most caring person I know and you want to help her, but it really isn't our problem."

"But are we obligated to report it in case she doesn't? I mean, did we leave the scene, in the eyes of the law?"

"Not if you weren't involved. But we should report it in case she didn't. Is it blocking the road?"

133

"No, it's in the ditch. Let's wait a half hour or so and give her a chance to report it herself."

She could see that he was reluctant but he agreed, looking at his watch.

"We had planned to make reservations at the restaurant for tonight but we took off in such a hurry—" she said.

"We'll just call. I'll check with the others—or did you girls already decide on a time?"

"No, not really. I'm going to put the laundry away and then fix a salad for lunch. Do you want a sandwich or anything?"

"I'll fix it, and after lunch we'll call the sheriff."

"Sounds fine."

THEY TOOK THEIR LUNCH out to the picnic table and joined Rob and Donna.

"What happened to Brandee?" Donna asked, scanning the celebrity encampment.

Frannie shrugged. "I don't know. I was telling Larry what happened and looked out, and she was gone. I hope she reported the accident."

"She said she didn't have any insurance and can't afford to get that car fixed," Donna said.

Rob shook his head. "From what I've seen of it before the accident, it's probably not worth fixing."

"No insurance?" Larry asked. "That right there is a violation and from your description, she couldn't pass a breath test either. We may have seen the last of her."

Jane Ann frowned. "Where would she go? I mean without a car?"

"I'm sure she went back to her RV. Maybe she'll phone a friend or someone in the group will help her. Not much point in guessing. We'll find out after lunch. Now what time do we want to go to supper? The girls think we may need reservations."

CHAPTER FIFTEEN
FRIDAY AFTERNOON

AFTER LUNCH, LARRY AND FRANNIE were delegated to visit the celebrity encampment and find out what had happened to Brandee. When they came back out of the camper after their cleanup, Mickey said, "The sheriff just pulled in over there."

"Hard to tell which crisis that is about." Larry rubbed his crew cut. "I bet that guy will be glad to see this week over."

MOST OF THE CAST and crew seemed to be milling around. A heavy, dark haired man brandished a clipboard and talked to the cast one at a time. The sheriff was talking to Shirley Joseph. Larry and Frannie joined them.

"Have you folks seen anything of Brandee Tudor? We found her car cracked up over on the Upper Falls road," the sheriff asked.

"That's what we came to talk to you about," Larry said and nodded at Frannie.

Frannie took a deep breath. She would just give the basic facts, but answer any other questions honestly.

"We came on her accident shortly after it happened. Me, my sister-in-law, and our friend Donna. Brandee wasn't hurt, so we gave her a ride back here."

The sheriff stuck his hands in his back pockets. "So, did you see where she went?"

"No," Frannie said. "I took my laundry in my camper, and when I came back out, she was gone."

"No one over here has seen her either. Had she been drinking?"

"Yes."

"Was she drunk?"

Frannie sighed. "I'm really not qualified to say. Legally, I mean. Maybe the bartender could give you a better idea of how much she had."

Sheriff Elliot pushed his hat back and scratched his head. "Without a breathalyzer test, I couldn't do much anyway. If you see her, tell her I want to talk to her. I'll have the car towed to the county impound." He tipped his hat and left.

Shirley turned to them. "This is very strange."

"It sure is," Frannie said. "Where would she go without any transportation?"

Shirley shrugged. "Into the woods?"

"She didn't strike me as an outdoorsy type. Is that guy the new producer?" She pointed at the large man with the clipboard.

Shirley rolled her eyes a little and nodded. "Baird McKewn. He's got a pretty tough rep. Not as nice as Cliff."

Tommy Pratt joined them. "What was the sheriff doing here? Any news about Cliff?"

"Brandee Tudor seems to be missing," Larry said. "Have you seen her this morning?"

"You're kidding. No, I haven't seen her since last night. She was pretty miffed about not taking over for Cliff. McKewn will do a good job, though. Brandee probably just took off somewhere."

One of the cameramen, Wyatt, came over to the group. "Mr. Pratt? Can I get an interview?"

"Sure. Where?"

"Let's go over by those trees."

Frannie watched Wyatt situate Tommy with one foot on a stump, elbow on his knee. He spoke to Tommy briefly, and then Tommy began to talk. His face showed anger, and he gestured and pointed with his other hand.

She moved a little closer, picking up a paper plate and beer can from the ground to throw in the trash. One can still be environmentally conscious even when being nosey.

Tommy's face reddened as he said, "…so they didn't have to bring in that jerk. Several of us could have handled the direction…" He certainly didn't sound convinced of McKewn's abilities on camera.

Shirley Joseph came up behind her. "Eavesdropping?" she whispered.

Frannie smiled as they walked away from the filming and headed toward the main group. "Just curious as to how this all works. Do they tell you what to say in these interviews?"

"Not really. But if there's a conflict going on with another character, they do their best to encourage that."

"So did Tommy really hope to take over from Cliff?"

"Maybe. He's done some directing and producing."

"Anybody else that wanted Cliff's job?"

"Well, Brandee, of course, and Gerard Fellows talked about it. Why?"

"The sheriff talked like maybe Cliff was murdered. I was just wondering who might have a motive."

Shirley's eyes grew wide. "Really?"

Frannie shrugged. "It just seems odd that Cliff was over by the lake. We saw him arguing with someone earlier and the next time anyone sees him, he's in the lake."

Shirley stopped walking. "I can tell you why he was over there. He went every morning to meditate. He loved the cliff area — no pun intended."

"Did everyone in the cast know that?"

"I don't know. I —"

She was interrupted by Tassi Ketchum's rather shrill voice. Tassi pointed toward Larry. "*Those* people were helping us. That was Brandee's idea. I don't think Cliff would have —"

"Cliff isn't here, and neither is Brandee." Baird McKewn's voice was surprisingly high and thin for his size. "But I would agree with Cliff. We don't need any outsiders mucking this up any worse."

Larry heard the comments also and beckoned to Frannie. "I think it's time for us to leave."

They walked back toward their campsite.

"We should have mentioned the drone to the sheriff," Frannie said. "I forgot about it."

"Maybe if he asked them for the film, they included that."

Frannie shrugged. "I'm convinced that someone followed Cliff that morning and pushed him off the rocks into the lake. I was in the tent area and there were several people I didn't see—Gerard, Brandee, Tommy. Either Tommy or Gerard could have been the person we saw arguing with Cliff earlier. And you know what? It could have been Brandee, too. She's got that stocky build. What?"

Larry had stopped and studied her. "You were in the tent area that morning? Why?"

Ooops. She hadn't mentioned that to Larry, only Mickey. "I walked Cuba that morning and took the path to see how the tenters made it through the night. I taught Tassi how to start a fire."

He continued walking. "I bet that was entertaining. But after our lectures the night before from Brandee and Cliff, you could have been asking for trouble going down there."

"Well, neither of them were there."

They reached their campsite. Donna and Jane Ann were setting out the dominoes.

"Just in time. Wanna play?" Jane Ann asked.

"I'll pass," Larry said. "I'm going to watch golf with Mickey"

Mickey looked up from his *Gourmet* magazine. "I'm watching golf?"

"Of course you are. You're the one with the satellite."

"Right," said Rob. "I'll bring the snacks."

Mickey sighed and hefted himself out of his chair. "The sacrifices I have to make for my friends."

Jane Ann rolled her eyes. "How about you, Frannie?"

"Sure, I'll play. Just give me time to get a glass of tea."

"Then you can fill us in on what you learned," Donna said.

Frannie did, although it wasn't much. As the game progressed, with Frannie getting trounced every time, the sun disappeared behind clouds and the breeze picked up. They took a break to get jackets and when they returned, they stirred up the campfire that had died down for lack of attention.

"You can tell that fall is upon us," Jane Ann said.

While they were picking up the dominoes, Donna said, "There goes the sheriff again."

He gave them a little wave as he passed their site. They watched him continue on around to the celebrity campsite. Filming activity had continued all afternoon, with the new director in evidence with his high voice carrying across the campground. The women watched as the sheriff's car pulled in, and he got out. The actors stopped what they were doing and gathered around him.

When the crowd parted, Frannie said in surprise, "I think he's arresting Tommy."

Sure enough, the sheriff ushered Tommy Pratt in handcuffs to the back seat of his cruiser and drove away.

"That's just wrong," Donna said.

Larry came outside to get a beer out of his cooler and noticed the women watching the actors' campsite.

"Now what?"

"The sheriff just came and arrested Tommy Pratt," Jane Ann said.

Larry frowned. "Evidently, he picked up something from his interrogations or the film. Looks like the director is giving them a break."

"Here comes Shirley Joseph," Frannie said.

Mickey and Rob had joined the group. Mickey rubbed his hands together. "I hope she's bringing baked goods." He quit when he caught a look from his wife. "Just sayin'."

"What's going on, Shirley?" Frannie said. "Here, come sit by the fire. The wind is getting chilly."

"It is." Shirley took a seat in the offered lawn chair and held her hands out over the fire. "I suppose you saw that they just arrested Tommy Pratt for Cliff's murder." She looked around at the group. "I know you've talked to the sheriff quite a bit. Do you know why they think he's guilty?"

"No, Sheriff Elliot is pretty closed mouthed," Frannie said.

"Did Brandee ever turn up?" Donna asked.

Shirley shook her head. "No one's seen her. I just don't understand about Tommy. He wouldn't hurt a fly. Gerard is going to find him a lawyer."

"We—Mickey and I—saw Cliff outside arguing with someone that morning. And another woman saw Cliff at the lakeshore arguing with someone, too. When I was on my walk, I went to the tent area, and I've been trying to remember who wasn't there. I mean, it must have happened about that time. I didn't see Tommy. And if it was him, how did he get back to the campground? He doesn't have a car here, right?"

Shirley shook her head. "None of us do, except the staff."

"Have any of them loaned anyone a car while you were here?" Rob asked.

Frannie nodded. "Good question."

But Shirley shrugged. "I have no idea."

"Apparently Tommy was one of the ones who hoped to take over for Cliff? And Gerard told me last night that Cliff had pulled out of one of Gerard's projects that he had promised to back. He wasn't very happy about that. And of course, Brandee. Seems like there's plenty of suspects."

"What about Cooper Wainwright?" Donna asked. "We saw him arguing with Cliff—probably over Tassi."

"Good point," Frannie said. "I didn't see him in the tent area either."

Larry sat at the picnic table with Rob and Mickey. He shook his head. "Ladies, I'm sure the world needs your

143

sleuthing skills, but the sheriff wouldn't have arrested Tommy if he didn't have good cause. They have to have some basis for bringing charges."

"Don't be so condescending," Frannie said. She lowered her voice and said to the women around the fire. "My money's on Brandee until we find out what happened to her. She's great and pleasant one minute and crabby and demanding the next. I wouldn't put anything past her."

Shirley shook her head. "What about a stranger? Seems more likely than someone here being able to get to the lakeshore."

Frannie considered that. She didn't like trying to use her sleuthing skills if the culprit was a complete stranger. What fun was that? So she was biased. "I think most murders are committed by someone the victim knows. But you're right—that's a possibility too."

"Get back to Brandee," Donna said. "She disappeared this morning after her wreck. We know she wasn't sober and all she had was her purse. No one saw her come back to her RV, right, Shirley?"

Shirley nodded.

"So where could she go? Cut through the woods to the road and hitchhike, maybe?"

Jane Ann added another log to the fire. "Hey!" Mickey said from the table. "Don't mess up that fire!"

Jane Ann stuck out her tongue at him. "Where's the nearest bus station or airport, I wonder?"

"Marquette or Sault Ste. Marie?" Rob said.

"Neither is very close." Frannie got up and walked out to the road. "The quickest way out of the campground from here would be those woods." She pointed to the east.

Shirley joined her and they crossed the road to an empty campsite and behind it, forest.

"It's really thick through here," Frannie said.

Shirley moved farther north. "Look over here. Someone's been through here recently."

Branches were broken or pushed aside leading down into a ravine. Frannie shuddered. "I don't think I'll follow the trail, but I bet you're right. She went this way." She shook her head. "She must have been pretty desperate to get away."

They turned and walked back to the campsite. The wind whipped around and Frannie pulled her jacket tighter. The lowering clouds mirrored the state of mind that she envisioned Brandee had been in when she took off that morning.

CHAPTER SIXTEEN
FRIDAY AFTERNOON AND EVENING

DONNA AND JANE ANN were picking up the dominoes when Shirley and Frannie got back.

"I'm ready for a hot shower," Donna said. "Are you guys dressing up for supper tonight?"

Frannie and Jane Ann looked at each other and laughed. "In what?"

Donna looked flustered. "Oh. I forgot we were camping."

"I'm going to wear clean jeans," Frannie said. "You know, since we got our laundry done."

Donna clapped her hands and her eyes sparkled. "You know what we should do sometime when we're camping? Go to a thrift store and pick out entire outfits for each other. Then go out to eat and then the next day, donate it all back."

Frannie and Jane Ann looked skeptical, but Shirley said, "That does sound like fun. Like one person could pick out all of the tops, another do skirts or pants, and another do accessories—without knowing what the others are choosing. What a hoot!"

"Yes!" Donna said.

"Maybe," Frannie said, "But let's do it someplace where we're a little closer to civilization. That hot shower sounds good. Shirley, would you call the sheriff about the path that we found? I think he's tired of my suggestions."

"Will do. I'd better get back in case our break is over." She laughed. She really didn't care.

AFTER HER SHOWER, Frannie decided she should 'dress up' a little. So after she put on clean jeans and a denim shirt with her favorite boots, she added a hand-woven blue plaid scarf and copper earrings she had gotten on a New Mexico trip. After days of her regular camping attire, she felt pretty spiffy. She was glad she did. Jane Ann wore a bright Mexican poncho, leggings and boots, and Donna had on one of her new lace shirts and a beautiful embroidered sweater with her jeans.

Larry whistled when they emerged from their respective campers and said to Rob "We'd better take both trucks. I think we'll be in trouble if we try and cram them all in one when they're decked out like that."

Frannie laughed. "We must look pretty bad most of the time."

Larry put his hands up. "Not goin' there. Hop into your chariots, ladies."

When they arrived at the Motley Moose, Madelyn and Chet Mays were waiting for a table.

"Why don't you join us?" Frannie said.

Madelyn smiled. "Well, if you really wouldn't mind, that would be great."

147

"No problem. Love to have you. We've thought about hosting ourselves and we can pick your brains."

Larry went to the desk to change their reservation.

They were soon seated and ordered drinks. Larry, Rob, and Mickey ogled the 'trophies' on the walls and the rest of the decor. Madelyn explained that the restaurant and other concessions were owned by the family who had donated the land for the park.

"Sounds like a smart financial move," Mickey said.

Frannie turned to Chet and Madelyn. "I suppose you know that Tommy Pratt was arrested for Cliff's murder?"

Chet nodded. "The ranger told us that Cliff was shot, and Tommy Pratt had a gun registered to him that matched the kind of bullet used."

"Interesting," Larry said, as he passed the basket of rolls. "We never heard how he was killed. So the bullet actually matched the gun?"

Chet shook his head. "They haven't found the gun. Tommy claimed it was stolen out of the RV he was assigned to."

"Did he report it?" Frannie asked.

"Unfortunately not, if that actually happened," Madelyn said. "He claimed he didn't know it was gone until the sheriff asked him for it. But he swears he had it when he got here."

"Was he sharing the RV with anyone?"

"Gerard Fellows. And Cliff had all of the keys," Madelyn said.

The waitress set salads in front of each of them. Mickey slathered his roll with butter, ignoring a stern look from Jane Ann. "Sounds like pretty flimsy evidence against Tommy."

Chet agreed. "But I think the sheriff is faced with the fact that these people are all supposed to leave in a couple of days, and he either has to sequester them in the park or solve the case. It might be wishful thinking."

"I can't figure how he got to the lakeshore to do the deed. He had no transportation, unless he stole something. And I'm really concerned about Brandee's disappearance," Frannie said.

Madelyn cocked her head. "Disappearance? I didn't know about that."

Frannie and Donna took turns relating the events of the morning. Frannie ended with, "So she left while I was in the camper and no one's seen her since. I found a spot in the woods — behind that last row of campsites — where it looked like someone had gone through recently, but I can't imagine where she would go. And why?"

"Poor girl," Madelyn said. "I talked to her quite a bit before you arrived and she's gone through some pretty tough times. Divorced recently and very broke. She was really hoping that this project would lead to some better things. Then if she was fired, that dream blew up. I don't know how that car of hers keeps running."

"Well, it isn't any more, after her accident this morning," Jane Ann said.

"True that."

149

The waitress brought their meals. Larry eyed his breaded whitefish with approval. "Time for a change of subject. I'd like to know more about your experience hosting. Do you like it?"

Madelyn nodded, her mouth full, and deferred to her husband.

"We do. This is our third gig. We were in Tennessee last spring and at a KOA last year."

The discussion continued with questions from everyone about the pros and cons and the dumbest things that they had seen people do.

Frannie wiped her eyes after laughing at one story. "I don't think it's mean to laugh. We've done most of that stuff ourselves. I don't know why camping seems to shut down our brains sometimes."

Mickey said, "Couldn't be the wine or beer?"

"Unfortunately, Mick, I think we've been stone sober when we've made the worst mistakes, so we can't even use that excuse." Frannie laughed and the others joined her.

It was a pleasant evening, one that Frannie polished off with a piece of pecan pie with ice cream, Mickey with apple pie, and Donna with a deadly looking piece of chocolate layer cake. The others abstained and made self-righteous comments about taking care of their health.

"Oh stuff it," Frannie said. "It's our last night here. And what if it was my last night on earth? It's the way I would want to go." She licked a glob of gooey pie filling off her finger.

"Well, *that's* morbid," Jane Ann said.

BACK AT THE CAMPGROUND, they stood for a few minutes outside discussing their departure plans. The persistent wind and chill didn't encourage more than a few minutes.

"We only have a three to four hour drive tomorrow, right?" Rob asked.

"Yeah," Mickey said.

"I propose a departure time about 10:00. We can break the drive halfway for lunch and still be set up by mid-afternoon. Won't have to rush around in the morning that way."

"Sounds good to me," Larry said. "What's the forecast, Mick?"

"Like this afternoon. Cloudy and cool but no rain. We'll have a headwind, though."

Larry grimaced but not for long. "Could be worse, I guess. See you all in the morning."

Inside, as they were getting ready for bed, Frannie said, "The more I think about it, the more I wonder if Brandee's strange behavior and then dropping out of sight isn't connected with Cliff's murder. She did have transportation to the lakeshore and probably had access to the RV keys. She could have taken Tommy's gun and she had motive."

Larry folded up his sweater and looked at her. "I think this time your judgment is being clouded by the fact that you like Tommy better than Brandee. I know that Chet thinks that the sheriff maybe rushed to make an

151

arrest, but the sheriff knows that he has to have evidence to bring charges and make a case. I think you have to let it go."

"You're probably right."

CHAPTER SEVENTEEN
SATURDAY MORNING

FRANNIE SLEPT IN the next morning and was awakened by a frantic pounding on the door. As she shook herself awake and sat up, trying to get her bearings, she heard Jane Ann yell, "Larry! Wake up!"

Frannie hurried to the door and opened it. Jane Ann stood shivering in her pajamas.

"Come in! You're freezing. What is it?"

"It's Mom." Jane Ann started to tear up and then shook her head and continued. "They took her to emergency this morning. They think it was a heart attack, and she isn't responding well. Is Larry up?"

"No, I'll get him. Sit down a minute. I'm so sorry to hear that."

Larry took longer to appear than she had. While they were waiting, Frannie plugged the percolator in and gave Jane Ann a jacket. She also turned on the space heater to take the chill off. Finally Larry emerged from the bedroom.

"Where is she?" Larry asked, as he pulled a sweatshirt over his head. It came out 'Wareshey?'

"At the University. They're saying she's in critical condition." She looked up at her brother with red eyes.

"Who called?"

"Elaine. She's already there." Jane Ann sniffed and wiped her eyes. "Bob is flying up and should be there by noon today. But it'll take us two days to get back, won't it? That's what Mickey thinks."

"I don't think we could do it in one—not with the campers." He thought a moment. "You and I could take the truck and leave the rest here. Then come back. Or possibly we could fly, but as remote as this is, it might take almost as long."

"No," Frannie said. "I wouldn't stay here when your mom is in the hospital. I'm sure Mickey wouldn't either."

"Well, then we could all four go in the truck and come back for our campers later. Rob and Donna could follow or continue the trip if they want—whatever."

Jane Ann shook her head. "I don't know, Larry. What if we are delayed a couple of weeks in getting back here for the campers? One more thing to worry about." She didn't say what could cause that delay, but they all knew.

Larry got a coffee mug out of the cupboard and poured himself a cup. He sat at the front edge of his recliner. "So let's just plan on leaving as soon as we can. We were going to leave about 10:00 this morning, right?" He looked at his watch. "I can be ready to hook up by 8:00 or 8:30. Frannie, is that doable for you?"

"No problem."

He looked back at Jane Ann. "That would probably work for you guys, too? Doesn't take you as long as it does us."

"Yeah, sure."

"I wish I'd gassed up the truck yesterday. I'll have to make a stop the first place we see. If we go eight or nine hours today, we should be able to be there by noon tomorrow. Unless we want to go longer than that today."

Jane Ann got up. "Let's see how it goes. It's only 6:30 now. I'll wait til 7:00 to see what Rob and Donna want to do." She hugged her brother. "Thanks."

"I haven't done anything yet."

"You made a plan. I feel better."

LOW, GREY CLOUDS combined with a stiff breeze to signal an end to the sunny fall weather they had enjoyed the last couple of days. It also made the necessary packing up less pleasant. Frannie took care of the inside tasks as usual to prepare the trailer for travel while Larry packed away the grill, chairs, side tables and other outdoor paraphernalia in the storage compartments and back of the truck.

When Frannie finished inside, she turned off the water heater and closed the slide extensions.

Mickey and Jane Ann were ready. Their class C motor home did not require as much preparation to get on the road. "We'll head to the dump station and then be out of your way. Latest message from Elaine says no change."

Frannie helped raise the stabilizers at each corner of the trailer and then directed Larry as he backed the truck toward the hitch. They completed the hookup, removed the wheel brakes, and did a final check. Donna came over to report that they would be ready to go in about ten minutes.

"I think I'll go hit the restroom while we're waiting," Larry said. "Nerves are playing havoc with my stomach."

"TMI," Frannie said. She noticed her little 'Happy Campers' garden flag was still stuck in the ground by the road, so she pulled it out and took it around to the driver's side of the truck to put it behind Larry's seat.

"Don't make a sound."

She jumped and immediately felt something jabbing her in the back. "What —? Who is it?" She tried to twist around to see behind her.

"You're going to get me out of here." It was Brandee. "This is a gun in your back, in case you couldn't tell. Unhook that trailer."

Frannie froze. She needed to stall. This woman was crazy. "I can't unhook it by myself."

A pause. "Fine. Then you'll have to pull it. Get in."

"But—I've never pulled it in my life—or any trailer," Frannie said.

"Get. *In.*"

Frannie turned slightly and saw the gun in Brandee's hand. "Maybe I can unhook it, and you can just take the truck…"

"I have nothing to lose. Get in." Her voice was low and cold.

Frannie pulled herself up in the driver's seat, grabbed the steering wheel, and leaned her forehead on her hands. What was she going to do?

Brandee opened the crew door, and Frannie heard her push the flag and various tools aside. She slammed the door and said "Drive."

Frannie glanced over toward Rob and Donna's trailer but another camper blocked her view. Ferraros had gone on to the dump station. She saw no one else out.

"Brandee, we got a message this morning that my husband's mother is very ill. We are headed home this morning, twelve hours away. Please don't do this."

"You *were* headed home. I don't *have* any family, so I guess I can't sympathize much." She actually laughed.

Frannie felt the gun barrel poke her in the shoulder, so she turned the key. She hated driving the truck because of its size and had no experience towing anything, let alone a thirty-foot trailer. And they needed to get home. This could not end well. She edged out on to the road—maybe if it took long enough to get going, Larry would get back and see her. . .

The road took a right curve toward the entrance. In her fear, Frannie didn't think about the trailer making the curve and the whole truck took a huge jolt as the trailer's right side tires dropped off the asphalt road and another jounce as the wheels returned to the road. Good thing it was only a slight drop.

Frannie gripped the wheel and bent over it. "Please, Brandee—I can't do this. We'll both be killed."

"Shut up. I have no choice. I need to get somewhere that I can take a bus or a plane or something out of this

God-forsaken place. Take a left when you get to the road."

Frannie concentrated on keeping the rig on the road. Fortunately there was no traffic and she could stay in the center of the narrow two-lane park road. Just past the check-in shack, they met a car—a compact even—but Frannie felt like the rig was taking over three-fourths of the road and there was no way they could pass. She held her breath and almost closed her eyes. They made it, but the tiny relief was overwhelmed by the realization that every vehicle she met would be the same horrible experience.

At the main road—still a two lane state highway—she prepared for a left turn, easier in her mind because she could see in the side mirror if the trailer was going to go in the ditch. She took a deep breath. No one was coming, so she gave the truck gas, jerking again as they pulled out. They bounced several times as they hit potholes. Maybe Brandee would drop the gun or get knocked out hitting her head on the window. Frannie could only hope.

"Brandee, if we could find a place off the road where we can't be seen, I think we could get this unhooked and then I could take you wherever you want—or you could just take the truck." Her emotion was so intense that her voice broke in the last sentence. That gave her such a feeling of hopelessness that tears started to run down her cheeks and fog her glasses. She thought about her crack the night before about her last night on earth. She couldn't really visualize Brandee as a killer, but she'd already killed once.

"I'll tell you what to do. Just keep driving."

"But we'd be less conspicuous."

Brandee laughed, a harsh, humorless sound. "Look around. There's nobody here. It doesn't matter if we're conspicuous."

"At least tell me where we're going."

"Marquette."

"Why are we doing this?"

"Sooner or later that sheriff is going to figure out that I killed Cliff."

Keep her talking, Frannie thought. Let her get it off her chest. "But why, Brandee? He seemed like a nice enough guy."

"This was my last chance. He warned me after I talked to you the first night that he might replace me with Tommy or Gerard. He wasn't interested in any of my ideas."

"They arrested Tommy yesterday afternoon for the murder."

Brandee's voice brightened. "Did they, now? Well, this is his gun. Too bad for him."

LARRY RETURNED FROM the shower house. His thoughts were on his mother and the long drive ahead. When he rounded the motor home in the next row from him, he stopped short. Rob walked up behind him.

159

"Hey, man, sorry to hear about your mom—Where's your camper? And your truck?"

Larry turned slowly. His face was pale and his eyes wide. "I have no idea." He couldn't say anything more. He glanced around the campground as if expecting it to appear.

"And where's Frannie?" he added softly. Mickey and Jane Ann pulled up along side their campsite.

"Shoemaker! What the hell? We just saw your rig leaving the campground, and it looked like *Frannie* was driving!"

Larry's jaw dropped open. "I don't know what's going on! Could you tell if anyone was with her?"

Mickey nodded. "It looked like someone was in the back seat."

Larry was still stunned. He looked from Mickey to Jane Ann and back to Rob and rubbed his crew cut.

"I bet it's Brandee. I should have listened to Frannie about her, but I thought she was harmless. Crazy, but harmless."

"Get in," Mickey ordered. "Bring Cuba." He pointed at the sad dog still tethered by the picnic table.

Jane Ann moved back to one of the dinette seats and Larry took her spot in the passenger seat. Cuba dropped at Jane Ann's feet with a sigh.

Rob had reached the passenger side. "Did you see which way they went?"

"No, we had just finished emptying the tanks, and it's too far from the entrance."

"Which way are you going to go?"

Mickey looked at Larry. "Uh, west, I guess."

"Okay. I'll unhook so I can go faster, and we'll go east." Rob put his hand on Larry's arm. "Frannie will drive as slow as possible, don't you think?"

"Hell, yes. She's really cautious even just driving the truck. She's never towed the trailer."

"We'll catch her. Call the sheriff!" Rob slapped the side of the door and took off for his rig, yelling for Donna.

Larry buckled his seat belt and pulled out his phone. He dialed 9-1-1 while Mickey pulled his motor home back out of the campground. He gave the dispatcher their location, a description of the truck and camper, and the license plate numbers. When he hung up, he looked back at Jane Ann.

"Anything more on Mom?"

"Not yet."

Larry threw his hands up. "You know what? I wasn't thinking. I'll call Rob and have him pick me up. You guys should head on home."

"No way," Jane Ann said. "I'll check in with Elaine and see how Mom's doing."

She placed the call, and reported back. "Mother is doing better. When Elaine told her what was going on, she told Elaine to tell us 'Don't come home without Frannie.'"

"Oh, man. You shouldn't have told them. She'll have another attack."

161

"How else was I going to explain that we were delayed?"

"Car trouble? Somebody's sick?"

"Neither of those would mean that the other of us couldn't get back. Just focus on your wife for now." Jane Ann ended with a little sob.

"What?"

"I just thought of what she said last night about the pecan pie…sorry. We need to stay positive. Frannie won't give up easily."

CHAPTER EIGHTEEN

LATE SATURDAY MORNING

FRANNIE *WAS* READY to give up. The sameness of the pines hemming in the road made her feel claustrophobic. Brandee hadn't seemed like a bad person and sometimes had been downright friendly. But right now she had tunnel vision about her career plans and financial woes and didn't care about anyone else. Frannie didn't get the sense that Brandee would have any reservations about shooting her.

She knew Larry would be already on the search. It wouldn't take long to notice that the truck and a thirty-foot trailer were missing. As well as herself. But what about her mother-in-law? Alice Shoemaker was one of the sweetest people she had ever known. Maybe Mickey and Jane Ann would go on back home and not wait for her to be found. She hoped so.

Her cell phone rang in her purse on the floor of the passenger side.

"Leave it," Brandee said.

"I couldn't reach it anyway." Could Larry track her phone? She had no idea, but there weren't many towers up here. Their reception had been spotty at best. They were lucky that Larry's sister Elaine had gotten through that morning; otherwise they would have no idea what was going on. Her morning coffee soured in her stomach as she pictured Alice in a hospital bed, hooked up to machines, and two of her four children stranded in the Upper Peninsula of Michigan.

What if something happened to Alice and her both on the same day? How would Larry cope? He was a really tough person, but he hid his emotions. He was right about her snooping — she had gotten herself into this. She asked Brandee too many questions. Her suspicions were obvious.

A loud buzz broke the silence accompanied by the low fuel warning light coming on.

"What is that?" Brandee shouted.

"The low fuel warning. We're about out. We'll have to stop the first place we see."

Brandee stuck the gun around in front of Frannie's face. "This better not be a trick."

"I can't make the dash light come on. It's not a trick."

"How long until we run out?"

"Honestly, I don't know. We're driving into the wind, and we go through a lot of gas when we pull this trailer."

Brandee spotted the atlas between the seats and pulled it out. It was quiet for awhile while Brandee flipped pages. She wasn't visible in the rear view mirror, but Frannie had to assume that the gun was still aimed at her back.

Brandee shoved the atlas back beside the console. "There might be something coming up in about twenty miles. We'll turn south and then there's a crossroads of two main roads. When we get there, slow down, but don't pull in until I tell you." Brandee was becoming calmer, more calculating. Frannie didn't know if she was scarier this way or when she acted wild and unpredictable.

"Okay."

She could feel the wind pushing against the truck already. She was terrified of turning south where the wind would be hitting them on the side. Maybe she wasn't strong enough to keep control and then what? She thought about her kids and grandkids. When was the last time she had talked to them? Or seen them? It had been the late summer for the grandchildren. They had taken Sabet and Joe camping and had a wonderful time. She felt like she had a vice on her heart. Sabet was entering her teens, but Joe was still at that wild energetic stage — always wrestling in the back seat and punching his sister. And then she had an idea — one that brought a small glimmer of hope.

"Do you have any cash?"

"What?" The question brought her out of her reverie with a jolt. Was this just going to turn into a robbery?

"Cash. I don't want you to pay for gas with a credit card."

"Oh. Um, I have some. Maybe forty dollars or so."

"We'll just get twenty or thirty dollars worth of gas then."

"I don't know if that will get us to Marquette."

"I'll deal with that. Just shut up and drive."

Frannie complied. Conversation with Brandee was a dead end. She hoped not literally.

The highway curved south, and she felt the wind buffeting the camper from the west, like a giant using the camper to play Crack the Whip. And the whip was the truck. She gripped the wheel harder and tried to concentrate. Fortunately the trees lining the road gave some protection, or it would have been worse.

She felt the muzzle of the gun at her shoulder again as they approached the crossroads and a gas station came into view. Good—it was on the right side of the road so she wouldn't have to make a left turn—something she didn't like to do even in her car. There were five or six pumps and only one vehicle there, a large new-looking pickup. She should be able to pull alongside the end pump without demolishing the whole island. Hopefully.

"Well?" she asked Brandee. "Should I turn in?"

"Yeah."

She made a wide right turn and edged up to the end pumps. She let out a huge breath as she turned off the key and started to reach over for her purse.

"Hold it! Hand me your phone first."

Frannie dug in her purse and brought out her old, battered phone. She handed it over her shoulder. "Now what?"

"Get your money out, and put your purse back on the floor."

Frannie did so.

"Okay, put thirty bucks worth in, and I will go in with you to pay when you get done."

"Okay." Frannie opened her door, slid out of the seat, and closed the door.

And ran.

She could hear Brandee shouting and pounding on her window. By the time Brandee reached over the seat to unlock the child locks—if she even thought of that—Frannie could be inside the convenience store.

She reached the doors and jerked on one just as a scruffy-looking man pushed it open from the other side and stared at her with surprise.

"Don't go out there!" Frannie yelled in his face. "There's a woman in my truck with a gun."

The man put his hands up, confused by her statement, and stepped back. Frannie turned to the clerk behind the counter, a middle aged woman with a badge that said "Dee."

"Can you lock those doors? That woman—" she looked out the doors to see Brandee already headed to the store waving the gun. She didn't need to finish. Dee reached under the counter and hit a button that caused a loud click from the double doors. But the doors were glass.

"Follow me," Dee said to Frannie and the scruffy man. She led them to an office, ushered them in, and locked the door. "I pressed the alarm button too. We should have help soon. The doors are break resistant glass."

She turned to the desk and swung a small screen around. The divided screen showed four views of the store. The pictures were black-and-white and there was no sound. The top two screens displayed the back door and the cash register area. Nothing was happening there. In the bottom left, an angry Brandee pounded on the glass doors, gun in hand. At the lower right, a grainy picture of the fuel island showed Frannie's camper and truck haphazardly parked, and, coming in the entrance, Mickey's Class C motor home.

"Oh my Lord—that's my brother-in-law!" Mickey parked on the far side of the pumps, and Frannie watched in horror as Larry got out of the passenger side and ran toward their rig. At the same time, in the lower left screen, Brandee turned, almost in slow motion, her gun aimed at the intruders.

"No!" Frannie covered her face.

"Good Lord, she's shooting toward the gas pumps!" Dee said and then breathed a sigh of relief. "There's the police."

Frannie uncovered her eyes in time to see a police cruiser screech to a halt near the other end of the fuel island from the camper. An officer jumped out of the driver's side and shouted at Brandee. He then took aim and fired at Brandee from behind his cruiser door. Brandee fell, clutching her leg. The officer and his partner approached her cautiously. They were shouting something. Frannie couldn't see Larry.

It was so frightening and yet so unreal—viewed through this silent fuzzy screen. Mickey started to exit his motor home, and one of the officers waved him back. But where was *Larry*?

Brandee rolled over and raised her gun, but her arm wobbled. The second officer fired and hit her shoulder. Her arm jerked, flinging the gun to the side.

The first officer spoke into his shoulder mike while the second picked up the gun. He handcuffed Brandee's wrists in front of her because of the shoulder injury.

"I've got to get out there!" Frannie said. "My husband —" She couldn't finish.

Dee unlocked the office door, and they headed toward the front doors. One of the officers was trying to open them, and Dee unlocked those as well.

Frannie ducked around the officer, stepped over Brandee, and ran toward Mickey, who was coming toward the store.

"Larry?"

Mickey pointed toward their truck. Larry stuck his head up from the other side of the hood and headed for her.

She turned and ran into her husband's arms. "We were watching from the security cameras and I didn't know where you went and Brandee was shooting and I thought—"

He pushed her back and grinned at her. "I had to see if you did any damage to the truck or the trailer."

169

She hit him in the arm. "Oh, stop." Now she was crying. "You were just trying to avoid being shot."

"Well, that too."

Mickey and Jane Ann came up, and both gave her a hug. Cuba jumped up and added a lick. "I hoped you guys would have gone on. What about your mom?" Frannie said.

Jane Ann wiped her eyes. "She's doing better, and she told Elaine to tell us not to come home without you, so we had no choice."

"Ohhh, she is so sweet." And Frannie cried harder.

By the time they answered the cops' questions and got back to the campground, it was another hour. An ambulance had taken Brandee to a nearby emergency room. Mickey called Rob to tell him the search was called off and the lost was found. Rob and Donna already had their camper hooked up again.

Several of the celebrities rushed over and congratulated Frannie on solving the case.

"I wouldn't have if she hadn't kidnapped me," Frannie said. "That was kind of a giveaway."

The new director asked if she would consent to an interview to be included in the pilot. She declined.

Sheriff Elliot came to return Tommy Pratt to the campground and freedom.

"How did Brandee get your gun?" she asked Tommy after he gave her thanks and a hug.

"When we got here Tuesday, I was putting my stuff away in the RV and it fell out of my bag. She was there at the time. And she obviously had keys to all of the RVs."

She turned to the sheriff. "And I kept forgetting to tell you that they were using a drone to do some of the filming. I didn't know if you knew that and had gotten access to it."

"We did. That was how we knew Tommy left the tent area that morning. It also showed Brandee's yellow car leaving the campground, but I didn't know that was her until she smashed it up."

"But you arrested Tommy anyway."

Elliot shrugged. "It was his gun. It would have gotten straightened out, so I'm sorry you had to go through what you did."

Frannie wasn't so sure, but kept her opinion to herself. "It's too bad we didn't think about Brandee being the one Cliff was arguing with that morning. She sort of has a shape and stance like a man, but I'd never seen her without a hat."

"Her back was to us and she was a long ways away," Mickey said.

"Well," Frannie said, "it's water over the dam—uh, waterfall—anyway. We're still headed home today, right?"

Larry nodded. "If you're up to it. We could stay until tomorrow if you need some recovery time."

"No, we should get back. Rob, what about you guys? Are you going to continue the trip?"

He shook his head. "No, we'll go back. What if we ran into another murder and didn't have you with us?"

"Oh hush." She turned to Madelyn Mays and Shirley Joseph. "It was so great to meet you guys. Madelyn, let us know where you host next. Maybe we'll run into each other again some time."

"That would be great." Madelyn gave her a hug.

Cooper, Tassi, and Gerard hugged her too. Finally they got loaded back in the pickup. Mickey and Jane Ann would lead.

Larry turned the key in the ignition and then grinned at Frannie. "Did you want to drive?"

"Get real," she said.

EPILOGUE

FIVE MONTHS LATER

A LATE SNOWSTORM HOWLED outside when the Ferraros arrived at the Shoemaker home. Frannie said, "Welcome! But hurry in so we can get the door closed." Jane Ann and Mickey shook snow off their coats and stomped their feet.

"Rob and Donna are already here." Frannie took their coats and hung them in the closet.

Jane Ann brought a tray of chicken wings and several dips. "You might need to warm those wings in the oven."

The pilot episode of *Celebrity Campout!* was being aired that night. The group decided they needed to watch it together. They didn't want to miss any opportunity to make fun of each other, and they didn't expect the portrayal to be flattering. That was why they had rejected Mickey's suggestion that they submit a news item about their adventure to the local paper. Everyone got their beverages and found a comfortable seat. Frannie had cleared the coffee table to hold the various snacks.

"At least if we embarrass ourselves, we can drown our sorrows in good food," Donna said.

Frannie smiled. "Larry's recording it so if we *did* embarrass ourselves, we can watch it again and again."

Mickey said, "Did everyone see the promotion today on that morning show?" They all had.

"They sure played up Cliff's murder, but didn't mention how Frannie caught the culprit," Donna said.

"I didn't actually. The police did."

"Well, Sheriff Elliot could have mentioned your part in it."

Shirley Joseph had emailed them that Brandee pled guilty to manslaughter and was currently serving a reduced sentence in Michigan.

"I wondered why they only charged Brandee with manslaughter, but the sheriff said they couldn't prove intention. Tommy Pratt knew she had seen his gun but didn't know when it disappeared. She may have taken it for a totally different reason," Rob said.

While they waited for the program to start, with some silly comedy muted on the TV, they discussed the upcoming camping season.

"We want to go back to the reservoir," Donna said. "That's such a great campground."

"And there's good shopping nearby." Jane Ann winked at Donna.

"Goes without saying."

"Remember several years ago when we were there and there was a balloon fest going on?" Rob said. "I think it was the third weekend in June. We should see if they're having that again this year."

Frannie nodded. "That *was* fun."

Larry turned the mute off. "Shh! It's starting."

They were instantly silent with eyes glued to the screen. The opening shots were short clips of the ice storm and climbing down the steps to the falls, interspersed with an interview of Tassi Ketchum, who discussed the pain of being on the set with Cooper Wainwright after their difficult breakup.

"Huh!" Mickey said. "She didn't *seem* that torn up about it."

"Hush," Larry said.

After several commercials for SUVs, drugs for psoriasis, and retirement homes , the program began with the arrival of the celebrities and tours of their luxury motor homes. Amber Gold was interviewed about her expectations. She gushed over the accommodations and reminisced about going to Girl Scout camp for three days when she was in sixth grade.

In the next scene, the participants were told that they were actually going to be staying in tents that they would have to set up themselves. Grumbling and anger rumbled through the group.

"They left out the food truck," Mickey said.

"Of course," Larry said.

The segment about setting up the tents was rife with conflict, especially when several found they were missing necessary parts.

Donna giggled. "It *is* funny."

The program continued with the next day in the tent area. Lots of complaining and mishaps. The narrator didn't mention that at the same time, the producer was dying a short distance away. After the next commercial break, a lengthy segment covered the ice storm.

In one shot, Larry pointed. "I think that's you, Frannie! It looks like your rain coat." A hooded figure scrambled around in the eerie light but was impossible to identify. They all then tried to find themselves, but it appeared that the editing had successfully avoided any other outsider appearances.

"Well!" Donna said. "I don't think there'll be any residual checks coming in the mail."

The hike to the waterfall the next day was a sunny contrast to the dreary scenes from the night before. The cameras followed the celebrities down the steps to gawk at the Upper Falls and then back up the stairs.

Frannie sat forward in her chair and pointed. "Did you see that? Brandee did push Jaqui!" They watched as Jacqui dangled, screaming. Brandee and Gerard tried to haul her back up. Larry and Jane Ann had rushed to help, but they were blocked from the camera view by the others.

"Why would she have done that?" Jane Ann asked.

"You know, Jaqui told me later that Brandee had left the morning before to get donuts right after Cliff left, but I didn't think anything about it until just now," Frannie said. "Brandee must have been worried that Jaqui would report that to the sheriff."

Expert editing also removed any shots of their group helping with the supper that night. When Cooper brought out his guitar, there were lots of nice closeups. Clips of the campfire singing while Mickey played never showed him, and since they followed the film of Cooper, viewers would assume Cooper was playing at that point too. The program went on with events of which Frannie and her friends hadn't been a part, and included some manufactured disputes and mishaps — at least they appeared that way. Interviews with fairly positive reviews of the experience ended the program. A dedication to Cliff Remboski appeared briefly on the final screen.

"Well, now we know why they never felt it was necessary to give us contracts."

"I think Brandee would have — at least, she said she would," Frannie said.

Larry frowned. "She also threatened to shoot you, and pushed Jaqui over the railing, so I wouldn't put a lot of stock in what she said."

"True. But I do wonder how she's doing. Such an unhappy person. Go back," Frannie told Larry. "Let's see that scene again on the steps with Jaqui."

Larry found the spot and they concentrated on the screen.

"I think you're right," Mickey said. "Would it help Jaqui to know that?"

Frannie shrugged. "Probably not."

Larry switched the TV off.

Jane Ann wiped her mouth and fingers after a particularly messy chicken wing. "I'd still like to go back up there and finish our trip. We didn't get to the 'Porkies' or any of the Wisconsin stops."

177

"Mom really appreciated us coming back, though," Larry said.

"Oh, I know, and I don't regret coming back when we did at all. I'm just saying I would like to catch those other sites."

Their mother had spent a couple of months in rehab with physical therapy and now was back in her own home. Whether she would be able to stay there remained to be seen.

"Well," Donna said. "I'd be up for that. And it should be less eventful. What else could possibly happen?"

THANK YOU...

For taking your time to share Frannie's adventures. Just as the sound of a tree falling in the forest depends on hearers, a book only matters if it has readers. Please consider sharing your thoughts with other readers in a review on Amazon and/or Goodreads. Or email me at karen.musser.nortman@gmail.com.

Find updates on my website at http://www.karenmussernortman.com on my books, my blog, and photos of our for-real camping trips. Sign up on my website for my email list and get a free download of Bats and Bones.

HAPPY CAMPER TIPS

Happy Camper Tip #1

Oven baked pork stew

1-1/2 pounds pork or beef stew meat, cut into 3/4-inch cubes

1 tablespoon cooking oil

3 cups beef broth

1/2 pound pearl onions or 2 cups frozen whole small onions

1 tablespoon snipped fresh oregano or 1 teaspoon dried oregano, crushed

1-1/2 teaspoons snipped fresh marjoram or 1/2 teaspoon dried marjoram, crushed

1 teaspoon lemon-pepper seasoning

1/4 teaspoon garlic powder

1/2 cup cold water

1/4 cup all-purpose flour

4 medium potatoes, cut into 1-inch pieces (4 cups)

4 medium carrots, cut into 1-inch pieces (1-1/2 cups)

1 cup fresh or frozen cut green beans

In a Dutch oven brown meat, half at a time, in hot oil. Drain fat from pan. Return all meat to pan. Stir in beef broth, onions, oregano, marjoram, lemon-pepper seasoning, and garlic powder. Bring to boiling. Remove from heat. Cover tightly and bake in a 325 degree F. oven for 45 minutes.

Combine water and flour; stir into stew. Stir in potatoes, carrots, and green beans. Bake, covered, for 1-1/4 hours more or until meat and vegetables are tender and mixture is thickened. Makes 6 servings. — Linda Miller

Happy Camper Tip #2

Banana Boats.
Make a flap in a banana and then a slit in the banana fruit itself. Fill the slit with marshmallows and mini chocolate chips. Fold the flap back over. Wrap everything in aluminum foil and put it on the fire for a few minutes. The best thing ever. — Julie Biver

Happy Camper Tip #3

Find Your Breakfast Hike
If you're camping with a bunch of little kids or even big kids, take those mini boxes of cereal and string them from trees or hide them in the woods a few minutes before you do the hike with the kids so they can find their own cereal while they hike and then you come back and have breakfast. — Julie Biver

Happy Camper Tip #4

Becky Ross Michael lived in the UP and found an old cookbook in the back of a drawer. The next three recipes came from there!

Pasties

Blend 3 cups flour, 1 ¼ cup vegetable shortening, ¼ tsp. baking powder and 1 tsp. salt to a coarse, crumbly mass. Add sufficient cold milk (up to ½ cup} to make dough that may be handled easily. Turn onto a floured surface and roll to leave fairly think. Cut into rounds measuring about 5-6 inches.

Cut 1 pound round or flank steak or ¾ pounds lean pork steak into small pieces. Dice 8 medium onions and 8 medium potatoes.(May substitute for part of the potatoes with turnips and/or rutabagas)

Place layer of onion on half of each pastry round, and then add layers of the other vegetables. Top with pieces of meat seasoned with salt. Fold over the other half of the pastry and moisten the edges to crimp together with a fork.

Place on baking sheet and cut holes for steam to escape. Bake at 425 just until the crust begins to delicately brown. Then reduce oven to 350 and continue baking for 1 hour.

Makes about 5 pasties.

Happy Camper Tip #5

Cry Baby Cookies

Mix 1 cup brown OR white sugar, 2 eggs, 1 cup vegetable shortening and ¾ cup molasses.

Sift together 4 cups flour, 2 tsp. cinnamon, 1 tsp. ginger, and ¼ tsp. salt. Add 1 cup raisins and 1 cup nuts.

Combine two mixtures while adding 1 cup warm coffee with 2 tsp. baking soda dissolved in it to blend. Drop by the spoonful onto a greased baking sheet.

Bake at 350 for about 10 minutes. Makes approximately 2 dozen.

For camping, you might want to try skillet cookies! Melt butter in your skillet and flatten each spoonful with a spatula after dropped in the pan. Cover and cook on low, turning as needed to cook thoroughly, about 5-10 minutes per side.

Happy Camper Tip #6

Pasta Sauce

Cook 4 slices bacon and 1 medium onion until the bacon is crumbly. Drain. Add 1 large can of diced tomatoes (with liquid), or 10 fresh, diced tomatoes and pinch of baking soda. Simmer. Add salt to taste. Serve with your favorite cooked pasta and grated cheese. Should make enough to accompany 1 small package of pasta. — Becky Ross Michael

Happy Camper Tip #7

On the Level

Sometimes on long trips you may be only spending one night at a campground. Your set-up and departure can both be much quicker if you don't have to unhook your trailer. But if you are level side to side and low in the front, what do you do to avoid sleeping with your head below your feet?   Use your leveling blocks under the rear tires of your tow vehicle.

Happy Camper Tip #8

For the record:

Carry a binder in your camper....include emergency contacts, medical info, medications, insurance, and doctor lists. Also, any pet info or proof of vaccines if you take a pet along. I guess any information that might be helpful in an emergency, — Susan Marie

Happy Camper Tip #9

Don't Get Caught Short!

I have not less than four first aid kits with me at all times! And I tend to use duct tape instead of bandaids. Because? Those bandaids are for when I help other people. (Not sure why my brain works like that!) — Alenia Lohnes

Happy Camper Tip #10

Stop!

Practice manually applying your trailer brakes by using the brake controller, so it is an automatic reflex to be able to find and apply your trailer brakes in case of an emergency. There are situations where one will need to do this and, in an emergency, you may not be able to find the controller quickly without looking for it. — Carol Jo Wood

Happy Camper Tip #11

Keep Cool!

I freeze two-liter bottles of water. Put them in your cooler or fridge (if your fridge doesn't work driving down the road) to keep things cool. Also, we freeze everything that is freezable before putting in the cooler. Meat, etc. — Nora Broadhurst

Happy Camper Tip #12

Easy as Pie

Sometimes you just need pie !!! Here is my favorite most simple pie recipe. Great for breakfast or dessert!

Impossible coconut custard pie

Ingredients: 2 cups milk, 1 cup coconut, 4 eggs, 1 tsp. vanilla, 1/2 cup flour, 6 Tbsp. melted butter, 3/4 cup sugar. Place all ingredients in a large bowl. Mix well and pour into a 10 inch pie pan. Bake @ 350 degrees for 45 minutes. Serve warm or cold.

Makes its own crust — Kim Patton Null

Happy Camper Tip #13

And for Pizza (Pie)

I love the old girl scout pie iron pizza, cooked over the open fire. 2 slices of bread, pizza sauce, shredded cheese, pepperoni and what ever other toppings you want. Spray bread with butter flavor Pam. Then for dessert use 2 pieces of sprayed bread and either cherry or apple pie filling. Cook in pie iron. — Cynthia Osterland Kinder

Happy Camper Tip #14

Fantastic Firestarters

My camping experiences revolve around campfires. We like to make emergency fuel ahead of time so we can start the campfire despite the conditions. Get paraffin from the canning section at the grocery store (or any wax you have). Melt the wax in a receptacle dedicated to melting wax. i.e. Old metal coffee can. Tear newspaper into narrow strips and roll the strips into a log shape. Take cotton twine and secure your newspaper log with the twine. Be generous with the amount of twine used to hold roll of newspaper in place. Leave a long tail of twine when you cut the twine free of newspaper roll. Take newspaper roll and dip in melted parrafin. Make sure you get the long tails of twine coated in wax. The long tails act like a candle wick. Use as many of these emergency fuels as needed to jump start your fire. When you melt the wax, be sure to use enough to easily saturate the newspaper rolls. — Ellen Haskell

I use old crayons, Scentsy wax and dryer lint. LOL Boy Scout mom. — Alenia Lohnes

I wrap pieces of candles in waxed paper, twisting the ends so it is easy to light. — Peggy Hietland Kaiser

I put dryer lint inside toilet paper tubes, then wrap the tubes in newspaper. Great fire starters. — Lorie Moorman

Happy Camper Tip #15

Veggie Paella in a Dutch Oven

Start coals using chimney, newspaper, and a lighter.

When coals are ready, place 8 or 9 coals in a circle. Place Dutch oven on top of coals. Add 1 Tbsp. vegetable or olive oil to oven. Add 1 onion chopped and cook until they become soft and clear.

Add 2 cups water, 2 vegetable bullion cubes, 2 tsp. dried thyme, 3 cloves of garlic, and 1 14.5 oz. can cut tomatoes and bring to boil.

Add 1 15 oz. can white kidney beans (do not rinse), 1 3 oz. can sliced black olives, 1/4 tsp. fresh ground black pepper, 1/2 tsp. (or less) salt, and 4 Tbsp. capers. Stir well.

Mix in 4 cups instant (one minute) rice and cover with lid. Place coals on top of lid.

Stir as needed. Add 2 bell peppers (any color) cut into squares when rice boils. Watch for steam to escape from Dutch oven. Stir one more time and remove from heat.

Let sit and then serve when ready. Serves 6 — Alenia Lohnes

Happy Camper Tip #16

Cowboy Beans

Lightly oil or spray Dutch oven.

In large bowl combine 1 15 oz. can baked beans,1 15 oz. can kidney beans, rinsed and drained, 1 15 oz. can Lima beans, rinsed and drained, 1/2 cup ketchup, 1/3 cup packed brown sugar, 2 tsp prepared yellow mustard, 2 tsp. cider vinegar, 1/4 tsp. salt.

Cook 1/4 lb. bacon, chopped (about 4 slices), and 1 onion, chopped over a full spread of coals until bacon is brown and onions are tender.

Move bottom coals to a ring around base of Dutch oven. Add bean mixture to Dutch oven, stir until well combined. Cover with as many coals as needed on lid to bring beans to a bubble. Simmer for 20 minutes.

Add 1 package smoked sausage (Kielbasa) sliced, cover and cook for 15-20 minutes or until sausage is heated through. Makes six 1 cup servings.

Happy Camper Tip #17

Jane Ann's Coleslaw

In a large bowl, toss together 1 (16 ounce) package shredded coleslaw mix, 1/2 large sweet onion chopped, 1 stalk celery chopped, 1/2 cup dried cranberries, 1/4 cup chopped walnuts, and 1 chopped tart apple. Mix 1/2 cup distilled white vinegar, 1/3 cup white sugar, 1/2 cup vegetable oil, 1 1/2 teaspoons salt, 1 1/2 teaspoons dry mustard, and ground black pepper to taste in a jar with a lid. Pour over the slaw mixture, and toss to coat. Refrigerate until serving.

Happy Camper Tip #18

Ojibway Falls State Park in *Real Actors, Not People* is based on beautiful Tahquamenon Falls State Park in the Michigan Upper Peninsula. The centerpiece of Tahquamenon Falls State Park's 50,000 acres is the Tahquamenon River with its waterfalls. The Upper Falls, one of the largest waterfalls east of the Mississippi, has a drop of nearly 50 feet, more than 200 feet across and a water flow of more than 50,000 gallons per second. Although many visitors come to this wilderness gem to see the falls, the park has many other places for you to explore and experience. The park has more than 40 miles of hiking trails, 13 inland lakes, 24 miles of the Tahquamenon River and approximately 20,000 acres of natural area. — Michigan DNR

The Great Lakes Shipwreck Museum is not far from the park and a very worthwhile stop. Then go west Munising and take the Shipwreck Tour and see the Pictured Rocks.

ACKNOWLEDGMENTS

Thank you is never enough. First I want to mention Nancy Kroes who gave us lots of hints when exploring the beautiful Michigan UP. Captain Theresa Karr of Shipwreck Tours in Munising, who pilots one of the glass-bottom boats, was very helpful and provided information about procedures in case a dead body is discovered caught on one of the wrecks. My Beta readers —Ginge, Marcia, Elaine, and Butch gave valuable feedback on all aspects of the book. Readers, especially members of the Midwest Glampers, sent me recipes and camping hints to share with you.

Fact check: Since fiction, by it's nature, isn't bound by the truth, I was rather liberal in moving locations to suit the story. Tahquamenon Falls State park, which is the basis for Ojibway Falls, is a short drive from Whitefish Point and the fascinating Great Lakes Shipwreck Museum. But the glass-bottom boat tours of the shipwrecks and the beautiful Pictured Rocks National Lakeshore are farther west and close to the town of Munising.

ABOUT THE AUTHOR

Karen Musser Nortman is the author of the Frannie Shoemaker Campground cozy mystery series, including the BRAGMedallion honoree, *Bats and Bones*. After previous incarnations as a secondary social studies teacher (22 years) and a test developer (18 years), she returned to her childhood dream of writing a novel. The Frannie Shoemaker Campground Mysteries came out of numerous 'round the campfire' discussions, making up answers to questions raised by the peephole glimpses one gets into the lives of fellow campers. Where did those people disappear to for the last two days? What kinds of bones are in this fire pit? Why is that woman wearing heels to the shower house?

Karen and her husband Butch originally tent camped when their children were young and switched to a travel trailer when sleeping on the ground lost its romantic adventure. They take frequent weekend jaunts with friends to parks in Iowa and surrounding states, plus occasional longer trips. Entertainment on these trips has ranged from geocaching and hiking/biking to barbecue contests, balloon fests, and buck skinners' rendezvous.

Sign up for Karen's email list at www.karenmussernortman.com and receive a free ereader download of The Blue Coyote..

OTHER BOOKS BY THE AUTHOR

Bats and Bones: (An IndieBRAG Medallion honoree) Frannie and Larry Shoemaker are retirees who enjoy weekend camping with their friends in state parks. They anticipate the usual hiking, campfires, good food, and interesting side trips among the bluffs of beautiful Bat Cave State Park for the long Fourth of July weekend — until a dead body turns up. Confined in the campground and surrounded by strangers, Frannie is drawn into the investigation. Frannie's persistence and curiosity helps authorities sort through the possible suspects and motives, but almost ends her new sleuth career — and her life — for good.

The Blue Coyote: (An IndieBRAG Medallion honoree and a 2013 Chanticleer CLUE finalist) Frannie and Larry Shoemaker love taking their grandchildren, Sabet and Joe, camping with them. But at Bluffs State Park, Frannie finds herself worrying more than usual about their safety, and when another young girl disappears from the campground in broad daylight, her fears increase. The fun of a bike ride, a flea market, marshmallow guns, and a storyteller are quickly overshadowed. Accusations against Larry and her add to the cloud over their heads.

Peete and Repeat: (An IndieBRAG Medallion honoree, 2013 Chanticleer CLUE finalist, and 2014 Chanticleer Mystery and Mayhem finalist) A biking and camping trip to southeastern Minnesota turns into double trouble for Frannie Shoemaker and her friends as she deals with a canoeing mishap and a couple of bodies. Strange happenings in the campground, the nearby nature learning center, and an old power plant complicate the suspect pool and Frannie tries to stay out of it--really--but what can she do?

The Lady of the Lake: (An IndieBRAG Medallion honoree, 2014 Chanticleer CLUE finalist) A trip down memory lane is fine if you don't stumble on a body. Frannie Shoemaker and her friends camp at Old Dam Trail State Park near one of Donna Nowak's childhood homes. They take in the county fair, reminisce at a Fifties-Sixties dance, and check out old hangouts. But the present intrudes when a body surfaces. Donna becomes the focus of the investigation and Frannie wonders if the police shouldn't be looking closer at the victim's many enemies. A traveling goddess worshipper, a mystery writer and the Sisters on the Fly add color to the campground.

To Cache a Killer: Geocaching isn't supposed to be about finding dead bodies. But when retiree, Frannie Shoemaker go camping, standard definitions don't apply. A weekend in a beautiful state park in Iowa buzzes with fund-raising events, a search for Ninja turtles, a bevy of suspects, and lots of great food. But are the campers in the wrong place at the wrong time once too often?

The Space Invader: A cozy/thriller mystery! The starry skies over New Mexico, the "Land of Enchantment," may hold secrets of their own. The Shoemakers and the Ferraros, on an extended camping trip, find themselves picking up a souvenir they don't want and taking side trips they didn't plan on.

We are NOT Buying a Camper! A prequel to the Frannie Shoemaker Campground Mysteries. Frannie and Larry Shoemaker have busy jobs, two teenagers, and plenty of other demands on their time and sanity. Larry's sister and brother-in-law pester them to try camping for relaxation-- time to sit back, enjoy nature, and catch up on naps. After all, what could go wrong? Join Frannie as "RV there yet?" becomes "RV crazy?" and she learns that going back to nature doesn't necessarily mean a simpler life.

A Campy Christmas: A Holiday novella. The Shoemakers and Ferraros plan to spend Christmas in Texas and then take a camping trip through the Southwest. But those plans are stopped cold when they hit a rogue ice storm in Missouri and they end up snowbound in a campground. And that's just the beginning. Includes recipes and winter camping tips.

Happy Camper Tips and Recipes: All of the tips and recipes from the first four Frannie Shoemaker books in one convenient paperback or Kindle version that you can keep in your camping supplies.

THE TIME TRAVEL TRAILER SERIES

The Time Travel Trailer: (An IndieBRAG Medallion honoree, 2015 Chanticleer Paranormal First-in-Category winner) A 1937 vintage camper trailer half hidden in weeds catches Lynne McBriar's eye when she is visiting an elderly friend Ben. Ben eagerly sells it to her and she just as eagerly embarks on a restoration. But after each remodel, sleeping in the trailer lands Lynne and her daughter Dinah in a previous decade — exciting, yet frightening. Glimpses of their home town and ancestors fifty or sixty years earlier is exciting and also offers some clues to the mystery of Ben's lost love. But when Dinah makes a trip on her own, separating herself from her mother by decades, Lynne has never known such fear. It is a trip that may upset the future if Lynne and her estranged husband can't team up to bring their daughter back.

Trailer on the Fly: How many of us have wished at some time or other we could go back in time and change an action or a decision or just take back something that was said? But it is what it is. There is no rewind, reboot, delete key or any other trick to change the past, right?
Lynne McBriar can. She bought a 1937 camper that turned out to be a time portal. And when she meets a young woman who suffers from serious depression over the loss of a close friend ten years earlier, she has the

195

power to do something about it. And there is no reason not to use that power. Right?

Trailer, Get Your Kicks!: Lynne McBriar swore her vintage trailer would stay in a museum where it would be safe from further time travel. But when a museum in Texas wants to borrow it, she determines that she must deliver it herself. Her husband Kurt convinces her to take it along Route 66 for research he is doing. What starts out as a family vacation soon turns deadly, and ends with a romance unworn by time. Travel can be dangerous any time, but when your trip involves the Time Travel Trailer, who knows where (or when) you will end up?

Made in the USA
Columbia, SC
15 November 2020

24628042R00121